Her Last Message

by

Ellen Shapiro

INDIES UNITED PUBLISHING HOUSE, LLC

INDIES UNITED PUBLISHING HOUSE, LLC
P.O. BOX 3071
QUINCY, IL 62305-3071

Other Novels by Ellen Shapiro

TRACEY MARKS MYSTERY SERIES

Looking for Laura

Secrets Can Kill

Missing or Dead

Memory of Murder

MADDIE LANDON MYSTERY SERIES

Buried in the Attic

Murder on Drake Street

A Dangerous Lie

For my daughter, Carrie, whose love and support fills my heart each and every day.

CHAPTER 1

I had just wrapped up a report for a client when I heard the front door creak open, followed by footsteps approaching my office. Instinctively, I reached for the gun tucked away in my desk drawer, keeping it close at my side. Moments later a woman stood before me, clearly upset.

"Are you alright?" I said, as I slid my gun back in my drawer.

"No, I need to speak with you immediately. Please, I don't have an appointment, but it's urgent. My daughter is missing," she said, her voice trembling.

"Let's sit, Ms…"

"It's Mrs. Dorothy Peterson."

"Can I offer you something to drink?"

"Maybe some water. My throat is dry." I filled up a glass of water and handed it to her.

"Were you referred by someone?"

"I don't remember. Does that matter?" she replied, her hands twisting nervously on her lap.

Mrs. Peterson appeared to be in her fifties, her small brown eyes reflecting a mix of concern and determination. Her pointed chin gave her a distinctive profile, while her mousy, curly brown hair was cropped short in an unflattering hairstyle.

"No, just curious. I don't get many walk-ins."

"I apologize if I seem a bit anxious; this is my first time speaking with a private investigator. As I mentioned, my daughter is missing and I'm absolutely frantic. I desperately need your help."

"I understand this must be incredibly difficult for you. Why don't you start from the beginning and fill me in?"

Mrs. Peterson took a deep breath.

"My daughter Katie recently called and left a message on my answering machine that I regret missing. When I got home it was too late to return her call. The next morning when I tried to reach her, I was disappointed when it went straight to voicemail."

"What did the message say?"

She played the message for me, her hands fumbling with the phone. "Mom, I'm going away for a few days. I need time to think about my marriage. I'll be in touch." Mrs. Peterson had tears in her eyes as she listened to the message.

"I've tried calling her back several times but she hasn't answered."

"What do you think your daughter's message meant?"

"Katie and her husband separated a few months ago. Maybe she's having doubts now," Mrs. Peterson said.

"Did she initiate the separation?"

"Yes. I thought it was a mistake, but she wouldn't listen to me." She paused, staring off into the distance. "I went over to her apartment yesterday thinking something might be wrong, but she wasn't home."

"Why do you think something may have happened to her?"

"It was her voice," she said softly. "I know my daughter, and something's not right. Katie's a teacher, and she wouldn't just leave her students. It's not like her to do something so impulsive. I don't understand why she didn't confide in me," she said, looking bewildered.

I had no idea if Mrs. Peterson was overreacting, but decided to keep that to myself.

"So, she never hinted that she planned to go away for a few days?"

"No, I would have remembered that," she said, frustrated.

"How long ago did she leave the message?"

"It was last Friday."

"You said you went over to her apartment. Was there anything you noticed that was different from the last time you were there?"

"Nothing that I can recall. I was so worried about Katie, my mind wasn't on anything else."

"That's understandable. Did you speak to any of her friends?"

"I only know her best friend Gail, and she hasn't heard from her in the past few days."

"What about her husband? Was she in touch with him?"

"I have no idea. She doesn't really talk about him. The last time I spoke with Paul, he mentioned he hadn't seen or talked to Katie in quite some time."

"How long ago was that?"

"About a week ago."

"Is there a reason why you're still in touch with her husband?"

"Well, sometimes he calls me to check on how Katie is doing."

I wondered if he was keeping tabs on his wife.

"Why are you asking me all these questions? I know something's wrong."

"I'm trying to gather as much information as possible regarding your daughter. I just have one more question. Did you go to the police?"

"I did, but I knew the detective wasn't taking what I said seriously. It doesn't make sense. Even if she did go away, why wouldn't she call me back? I just know something's wrong. I filled out a missing person report, but I didn't get the impression they're going to help me."

I could understand why the police would be skeptical.

"Can you tell me what precinct you went to and who you spoke with?" Mrs. Peterson took out a business card from her purse and handed it to me.

"I know Detective Marks," I said, looking at his card. "I used to be a detective with the NYPD. I'll make a call."

"Thank you, but that's not why I'm here. My husband and I want to hire you to find out what happened to our daughter. I don't think the police believe me and I need to know she's safe."

"Where's your husband now?"

"He's at work."

"Will he be home around 6:30? I could come by then since I'd like to speak to both of you together."

"Yes, thank you so much." Before leaving, Mrs. Peterson wrote down her address and contact information.

I thought about my conversation with Mrs. Peterson after she left. It was certainly understandable why she would be upset, but I just wasn't convinced that something happened to her daughter.

CHAPTER 2

Later that day, I drove from my apartment on the Upper West Side of Manhattan to Mrs. Peterson's home. Crestwood is a small community in lower Westchester County, with well-tended Colonials, Tudors, and Victorian single-family houses just west of the Bronx River Parkway. The Bronx River Parkway is a narrow, winding scenic road that was completed in 1925, designed to accommodate the Model-T, whose top speed was probably forty miles an hour. Much of the parkway remains unchanged.

The Petersons lived in a Tudor-style house on a small plot of land with flower boxes full of white and pink chrysanthemums outside of their second-floor windows. I rang the doorbell. When it opened, Mrs. Peterson was wearing the same canary yellow pantsuit that she had worn earlier in my office.

"Please come in. James, Ms. Landon is here," she shouted. The foyer was quite dark; from what I know about Tudors, they often have a dim interior. Mrs. Peterson led me into the living room.

"James, this is Ms. Landon." We shook hands. I sat down on a three-cushioned, beige overstuffed sofa with decorative pillows casually placed. It was quite comfortable. They sat opposite me on matching club chairs. Mr. Peterson was about the same age as his wife, with a medium build, weathered complexion and a full head of dark wavy brown hair.

"As I mentioned to your wife, I thought it would be best if I spoke to both of you together. Your wife seems to think something may have happened to Katie. What do you think?"

"I just don't know. It does seem out of character for her to just leave without telling us. Since she separated from her husband, I noticed she's been acting different lately."

"In what way?"

"The one thing that comes to mind is that she's been more distant lately, and we don't talk as much."

"Would you say you were close to your daughter?" I asked, trying to gauge his reaction.

"We both were," Mrs. Peterson interjected quickly, her voice almost defensive.

I couldn't help but wonder if there was something going on between them.

"Do you know why they separated?"

"My daughter is a very private person," Mrs. Peterson said, her gaze dropping to the floor. "We're not sure." Mr. Peterson remained silent, his expression unreadable. What wasn't he saying?

Since I'm not a mother, I had no idea if it was that unusual a daughter wouldn't confide in her parents about her personal life.

"Has Katie said anything to either of you recently that she was worried about something or if someone was bothering her?"

"She told me that her husband had been calling her lately, wanting to get back together. Other than that, I can't think of anything else," Mr. Peterson said.

"I didn't know that Paul was calling her," Mrs. Peterson said, her face slightly red as she glared at her husband. He just shrugged.

"Do you know if anyone at the school was harassing her?"

"If there was someone, she never mentioned it," Mrs. Peterson said.

"Is there anything you can remember? It might be something in passing that at the time you didn't think was important."

"As I said, everything seemed fine. You might want to check with her husband or her friend, Gail Davis," Mrs. Peterson said.

"One last question. Did you contact the school to find out if she had showed up?"

"Yes. They said she had called and told them she would be out for a few days—something had come up that she had to take care of. She never said anything to us," Mrs. Peterson said, with a worried look on her face.

"Do you know who Katie spoke with at the school?"

"It was Mrs. Roberts in the administration office."

Before leaving the Petersons, they signed a retainer agreement and provided me with the contact information for their daughter's husband as well as her best friend. Mrs. Peterson agreed to meet me at Katie's apartment the following day. I wanted to take a look around. Maybe I could find something that would give me a clue as to what may have happened to Katie.

CHAPTER 3

Driving home, I wasn't sure if the Petersons were being totally honest with me. I've learned from my years as a police detective and a private investigator that people hold back, whether it's because they have something to hide or because they may be embarrassed about revealing certain details. Whatever the case, it usually winds up spilling out at some point. Pressing them now, when their daughter might be missing or worse, was not in my best interest.

I arrived back at my apartment at 8:30 p.m. For the past twelve years, I've lived on the Upper West Side in a one-bedroom apartment on the third floor. Though my decorating skills have a lot to be desired, between a mix of my mother's antiques, interspersed with mostly modern furniture that I bought at Pottery Barn, my place is warm and cozy. I placed my keys on my favorite piece, a black medallion antique wood console that greets me in my foyer as I enter my apartment.

I quickly showered. While drying myself off, I noticed how all my running and hard work at the gym was paying off. I slipped on my boxer shorts and a T-shirt before peeking into the refrigerator in search of something to eat.

"Hey, babe," I said, when I saw it was Jesse calling.

"How's everything in the Big Apple?"

"Great. Just got a new case." I went on to tell him about it. Jesse is also a private investigator, who works for two criminal defense attorneys in Connecticut.

"Are we all set to look at some apartments on Wednesday?" Jesse said.

"We're meeting with the realtor at 10:00 a.m. She's scheduled a few places for us to see."

Jesse lives in a small brick house in a rural but very charming town on the Connecticut River. He completely renovated it, with a loft area that accommodates a bedroom, work area, and bathroom. Though I love the house, what I love most is hanging out on the back porch, where we barbecue when the weather allows. Us city folks don't have that luxury.

"What are you up to?" I said.

"We have a client who swears he was at a friend's house the night of a burglary. I have to check out the friend, since I'm not sure if he'll make a good witness, but even if I think he's lying, we might have no choice but to put him on the stand."

"I'm glad I don't have to represent criminals. When I was a detective, I liked putting away the bad guys."

"Did you forget that there are people who are accused and are innocent?"

Jesse was referring to a client of mine on my last case. A seventeen-year-old boy was accused by a classmate of rape. It turns out the accuser pointed the finger at my client because the person who raped her threatened harm to her family. In the process of finding the real rapist, I was almost killed. But what if I never found the person who raped her? If my client was convicted, he would have spent a good part of his life in prison. It made me think about all the other innocent people who were wrongly accused, convicted, and sitting in prison.

"I'll see you on Wednesday," I said to Jesse, keeping my doubts about moving in together to myself.

***

In the morning, I took the subway to meet Dorothy Peterson at her daughter's apartment in the West Village in Manhattan.

I love New York and everything about it, including the New York City subway system. It's an easy way to get around the city. My only problem is my fear of enclosed spaces. Every time I walk onto the train, my anxiety level shoots up, and every time the train stops for any reason, I start to worry, going over in my head all the scenarios why the train would come to a halt. None of them very comforting. Most of the time the conductor never tells us why we're waiting, and if he does, it's usually garbled, hard to understand. I breathed a sigh of relief as we rolled into the station without any complications. I walked the few blocks to Katie Lewis's apartment building, where her mother was standing outside waiting for me.

Katie's apartment was a small one-bedroom on the fourth floor. The furnishings had seen better days. The tattered brown couch was faded in spots, and the only thing that looked new was a 52" television hanging on the living room wall above a walnut credenza.

"What do you expect to find?" Mrs. Peterson said, following me around.

"I don't know. Can you tell me if she had an overnight bag or any luggage that might be missing?"

"I didn't think to look. Let me check her closet."

A few minutes later, Mrs. Peterson said that her daughter's overnight bag was gone. "That's good, isn't it? Maybe I overreacted and perhaps she did go away for a few days."

At this point, I didn't know what to think.

"Did you notice if anything else was missing?"

"Her cell phone and laptop are gone."

"Does anything look different from the last time you were here?"

"I don't think so. Again, it's been a while since I've been in the apartment."

I noticed a table with several photos. I picked one up.

"Is this your daughter?"

"Yes, that's Katie and me. She looks so happy there."

"How old is Katie?"

"She just had a birthday. She turned twenty-eight."

Katie didn't look anything like her mother. She was beautiful, with large brown eyes, high cheekbones, and a perfect nose. Her wavy, dark brown hair came down to her shoulders. I took a photo with my cell phone.

"By the way, does Katie drive?"

"She has a license, but living in the city it's difficult to have a car. Mostly she takes the subway or gets a cab or an Uber."

I quickly looked around, seeing no signs that Katie hadn't left of her own accord. I thought I would come back another time when I was by myself for a more thorough search. On our way out, I told Mrs. Peterson I would be in touch with her as soon as I had any news.

CHAPTER 4

Since I was only a few blocks from the elementary school Katie taught at, I walked over to see if Mrs. Roberts, the woman Mrs. Peterson spoke to, was available to talk with me.

When I arrived, the main entrance was open and I headed for the door marked **Administration.** Was it my imagination or were all elementary schools institutional-looking, both inside and outside, giving the hallways a cold feeling. As I walked down the hall, I remembered the class drawings that the teachers tacked up outside of their classroom for parent/teacher day.

"Excuse me," I said out loud to no one in particular. One of the women in the office came up to the counter and asked if she could help me.

"I'm looking for Mrs. Roberts."

"I'm Mrs. Roberts. How can I help you?" Mrs. Roberts gave off an air of authority that made it clear she was in charge. She was probably in her fifties, wearing a dress that was hiding a figure carrying a little too much weight.

"My name's Maddie Landon. I'm a private investigator," I said, handing her my card. "I was informed that you spoke with Dorothy Peterson regarding her daughter."

"Why yes. Is there a problem?"

"I'm not sure. Her mother said Katie left a message on her phone, and when she tried calling her back several times, Katie hadn't responded. Can you tell me exactly what Katie said to you?"

"Just that an emergency had come up and she needed to take a few days off. She was very apologetic she was giving us such short notice."

"Has she ever taken time off without giving advance notice?"

"No. Never."

"How did she sound to you? Did she seem upset?"

"I don't know, maybe like she was in a hurry, but I would say more like nervous or distracted. Do you think something has happened to her?"

"At this point I have no reason to believe that's the case. Is there someone at the school Katie was friendly with?"

"She and Paige always had lunch together. I'm not sure how close they were outside of school."

"Would it be possible to speak with her now?"

"Her class is over in about ten minutes. She has a break in between classes, if you wouldn't mind waiting?"

"Yes. That's fine."

"I'll call her room and ask her to meet you in the teachers' lounge."

"Actually, can we meet some place more private?"

"I guess it would be alright to meet in her homeroom. I'll call and let her know."

Paige Mitchell was about the same age as Katie. She was tall, thin, and dressed in a beige pencil skirt that came just below her knees, with a white blouse and a wide black belt. She looked very put together, a stark contrast to my jeans, white pullover sweater, and low-cut black boots; my standard work uniform. Paige had straight, light brown hair that she was wearing up in a bun. On Paige it looked sophisticated. My eyes did a quick glance around the room, bringing me back to my third-grade classroom. I recalled my teacher's name, Mrs. Wasserman. At the time she seemed old, but perhaps was only in her thirties, closer to my age now. Were the desks and chairs always this small?

"Hi, Paige Mitchell," she said, greeting me.

"Maddie Landon. I'm a private investigator." Her brows shot up.

"What's going on?"

"Mrs. Peterson, Katie Lewis's mother, is worried about her." I mentioned to Paige the phone call to her mother and the fact that Katie told the school she would be out for a few days because of an emergency. "Do you know what the emergency was?"

"I have no idea. Please sit. To tell you the truth, I'm surprised. She never mentioned she'd be taking off a few days."

"Were you two close?"

"That depends on what you mean by close. We have lunch together almost every day and talk about various things, but we don't socialize outside of school."

"Can you tell me why?"

"Just life. I have a young daughter who keeps me busy when I'm not here."

"What can you tell me about Katie?"

"She loves her students and is devoted to them. The kids adore her. If there are supplies that the school can't afford, Katie buys whatever her kids need out of her own pocket."

"Can you tell me what you and Katie talked about?"

"As far as I know, nothing's happened to Katie, so I'm uncomfortable sharing what she told me. She may have her reasons why she hasn't responded to her mother's calls."

I wonder what those reasons might be.

"I understand I've put you in an awkward position. Why don't we try it this way. I'll ask you some questions and you can share whatever you feel comfortable telling me."

"Look, I don't want to be difficult, but unless I know Katie's in trouble, I'd rather keep my conversations with Katie private."

I was frustrated. "Here's my card. If you change your mind, please call me."

"Wait," Paige said as I was leaving her classroom. "There is one thing. The last time I spoke to Katie, I got the feeling something was on her mind. When I asked her if everything was alright, she assured me everything was fine, but I wasn't convinced."

"Why not?"

"As I said, nothing I could pinpoint."

"Thank you. If you remember anything else, please contact me."

Walking out of the building, I was very curious what Katie Lewis shared with Paige. Whatever was going on with Katie, it appeared no one I spoke with so far had any inkling about her private life. Perhaps when I speak to her husband I'll know more.

CHAPTER 5

I took a taxi back up to my office, which is located in a brownstone about fifteen blocks from my apartment building on the Upper West Side. The first floor houses three offices: Mine, marked by a plaque on my door that reads, 'Maddie Landon, Private Investigator'; my cousin Will's insurance agency; and the third office occupied by a criminal attorney, Larry Banks. The upstairs has three rented apartments.

During my last case, a commotion in the hallway outside of my office caused by one of the tenants distracted the person who was trying to kill me for just a moment, and that split second saved my life.

First thing I did when I got in was contact Detective Marks at the 6th Precinct. After being on hold for what seemed like an eternity, Detective Marks picked up.

"Detective Marks, this is Maddie Landon. I was a detective out of the 20th Precinct a few years back."

"I believe we crossed paths on two homicides committed by the same person, but in two different jurisdictions," he said.

"Yes. Good memory. I'm calling because a woman by the name of Dorothy Peterson filed a missing person report on her daughter, Katie Lewis."

"As I recall, the mother was sure something happened to her, but there didn't appear to be any indication of foul play. I was told the daughter called the school and said she wouldn't be in for a few days. At this point, unless something else shows up, we have nothing to go on."

I didn't say anything.

"If the mother comes in with any additional information we'll look into it, but for now we don't have any reason to. Are you planning on investigating?"

"Though you may be right, I'll do some digging. But doesn't it seem a little odd that the daughter never returned any of the mother's calls?"

"We don't know the dynamics of the family. Maybe there were some problems."

"Then why call the mother at all?"

"That's a good point. Look, if you find anything that might be suspicious, let me know."

"Thank you," I replied and I hung up. That answered my question. Mrs. Peterson was right. Detective Marks had no plans of looking into Katie's disappearance, at least for now.

Though I sometimes wonder if I made the right decision leaving the New York City Police Department, I knew there was no way I could work my way up the ranks in an old-boy network. Working for myself gave me the freedom I didn't have on the police force.

I was getting hungry. I locked up and went to a local coffee shop, where I parked myself in a booth in the back and ordered scrambled eggs, toast, and coffee. The waitress, Sandy, knows me so well she practically places my order for me. While waiting, I Googled Katie's husband, Paul Lewis, with the address I had for him. Not much came up. Before calling him, I thought I would conduct an in-depth database search under his name when I returned to the office.

My mind wandered. Jesse and I were looking at apartments tomorrow. It took me a long time to even consider moving in with him, and now that it was becoming a reality, my fear of commitment loomed large. I hated that I couldn't let go of the past, and it still had such a strong hold on me.

"Can I get you anything else?" Sandy said, interrupting my thoughts, as she set down my eggs and coffee.

"No, thank you."

I quickly finished and went back to my office. The search I did on Paul Lewis failed to reveal anything out of the ordinary. He was thirty years old and worked as an assistant manager at a local bank in Riverdale, New York. I called his cell number and was about to leave a message when he answered.

"Mr. Lewis, my name is Maddie Landon. I'm a private investigator hired by Katie's parents. They're concerned that something has happened to their daughter, and I'd like to ask you a few questions."

"What's going on?" he said, his voice lifting a few octaves.

"Actually, it would be better if we could talk in person. Can we meet later?"

"It would have to be after work. There's a bar a few blocks from the bank. If you send me a text, I'll forward the info," he said, and hung up.

I was sitting at the Tortoise & Hare bar in Riverdale, waiting for Paul Lewis. Riverdale is an affordable alternative to the Upper West Side, located in the Northwest part of the Bronx. Above the bar there are two televisions, both with the sports channel on. I recognized Mr. Lewis right away from his brief description. He was maybe my height, 5 feet 8 inches tall, trim, dressed in khakis, a blue button-down cotton shirt and a blue blazer. He had a strong jawline with large almond-shaped blue eyes. His hair was cut short, military style.

"There are a few tables on the porch. Would you mind sitting outside?" I asked him.

"No, but I'm in a bit of a hurry."

It was a brick porch with square tables covered with red and white tacky plastic tablecloths.

"I'll try not to keep you too long," I said. Paul ordered a Budweiser and I ordered a glass of Sauvignon Blanc. "Have you been trying to get in touch with Katie?"

"How did you know that?"

"Katie's father said you wanted to work things out with her. Is that right?" Our drinks came. Mr. Lewis took a swig of his beer before answering.

"Yes. I just thought we gave up too early in our marriage."

"Can you tell me what the problem was?"

Mr. Lewis squirmed in his chair. "I'm not making excuses, but Katie and I had only been married for a little more than a year and she wanted to have a baby."

"And you wanted to wait?"

"Yes. I thought it was too soon. I wanted us to have the freedom to go places without worrying about a baby to take care of."

I had the feeling there was more to the story. "How long did you want to wait?"

"Maybe a year or two."

"Are you sure it wasn't anything else?"

He hesitated. "I would prefer if you didn't divulge what I'm about to tell you with her parents."

"You have my word."

"Katie would often go out late at night, returning around one or two in the morning, yet she never shared where she had been. I felt a distance growing between us, as if I couldn't reach her anymore."

"So it wasn't about a baby?"

"Not entirely," he said sheepishly.

"Do you have any idea where she went on those nights?"

"I don't. I thought maybe she met a friend and they went to a bar."

Why would he think she went to a bar? She could have been having an affair or gone anywhere for that matter.

"And you have no idea what was going on with your wife?" He shook his head.

"I've been calling her for the last few days with no response. I thought she didn't want to hear from me. Did something happen to her?" he said, looking worried.

"Katie's mother seems to think Katie might be in trouble. She contacted her school and said that something had come up, and she would be out for a few days. You need to tell me what you know."

"I don't have much to say. It's been over a month since I last saw Katie. When we did speak, I tried to encourage her to open up to me, hoping to rekindle our relationship, but she seemed uninterested."

"That must have hurt."

"Yes, but if you're thinking I did anything to Katie, you're wrong. I would never hurt her, no matter what. I'm sorry, I can't help you."

"What about friends?"

"I only know her friend Gail Davis. Maybe she can tell you where Katie is."

"Before I leave, is there anything else you can think of that might help to locate her?"

"I'm sorry, please just find her."

"By the way, do you think your wife was having an affair?" Paul's face turned red.

"I have no idea," he said in a bitter tone.

I gave Paul my card and asked him to call me if he heard from his wife. I wasn't holding my breath on that one.

CHAPTER 6

In the morning, I was outside my building waiting for Jesse. The temperature was sixty degrees, fairly warm for the end of October, but I couldn't stop shivering. I zipped up my leather jacket and pulled my scarf tight around my neck. Jesse was late for our appointment with the real estate agent. Part of me was hoping he had changed his mind, deciding living with someone with so much baggage wasn't going to work out. Even though I had finally agreed to move in with Jesse, I still had nagging doubts.

Jesse and I met almost two years ago at a Barnes & Noble on the Upper West Side, where we were both browsing the mystery section. I wasn't necessarily looking to meet someone—though I wasn't opposed to it—but it wasn't something that typically showed up for me. He asked if I had any suggestions for a good mystery, and I mentioned that I enjoy reading Michael Connelly. It was his eyes that caught my attention first; I had never seen such big, dark, alluring eyes. When he asked if I wanted to get a cup of coffee, I thought "what the hey." This was going to be a onetime encounter, so why not? Now, I'm standing outside, waiting for Jesse, getting ready to look at apartments.

I'm thirty-eight and never thought this day would come. How did I ever think this was a good idea? There was a part of me that realized if I didn't make that commitment, Jesse might decide to end our relationship. I knew this wasn't about him; it was my own fear of getting too close, knowing you can lose everyone you ever loved in an instant. Though it's not logical, it's what keeps me up at night.

Jesse waved as I saw him approaching. The broad smile on his face was enough to melt my heart, but was it enough to keep my fears at a distance.

"Hey, babe, traffic was a bitch this time of day. You're trembling," he said, as he wrapped his strong arms around me. "Is everything okay?"

"I guess I'm not dressed warmly enough," was all I could think of saying. "The agent said she would meet us upstairs." Jesse took my hand.

"Is it the elevator or the stairs?" Jesse said, knowing my fear of enclosed spaces.

"I'll brave the elevator." Once inside, I pressed the button for the fourth floor. Depending on how you look at it, I was either lucky or unlucky that a two-bedroom, two-bathroom apartment just became available in my building. I purchased my apartment with the money my Aunt Jenny left me. Aunt Jenny, my mother's sister, came to live with me after my parents died in a tragic car accident. I was in the back seat when it happened, and to this day, I still have nightmares that wake me up screaming.

"I'm Sarah," the agent said as we walked into the apartment. "And you must be Maddie."

"Yes, and this is Jesse." Sarah appeared to be in her forties, with short, curly red hair in a pixie style. Make-up added to her average looks. She was dressed in a black pantsuit with a bright red turtleneck sweater underneath. My interactions with realtors were nil, but from what I heard, they could be pushy.

"I guess I don't have to tell you about the building. It saves a lot of time," she said, trying to make a joke that fell flat. "The man who was living here was relocated for his job. An agency will be coming in to remove his furniture and have the place cleaned out. As you can see, the kitchen has been completely remodeled, all state-of-the-art appliances, new white wooden cabinets, and an island where you can sit and eat. What I like about the apartment is that the living room and kitchen area are one large room, which gives it a very spacious feeling."

Though Sarah was doing a good pitch job, my anxiety was getting the best of me. As she was showing us the rest of the apartment, I was appropriately nodding every so often. Jesse asked a question or two.

"What do you think?" Jesse said, after we went through the rest of the rooms with Sarah out of earshot.

"With Leo staying with us from time to time, we would definitely need two bathrooms, and we can make the second bedroom into an office/bedroom." Jesse recently found out that he had a five-year-old son, which was a shock to both of us.

Sarah showed us two other apartments, both on the Upper West Side. Jesse was partial to the one in my building since the kitchen and one of the bathrooms had already been updated. He also liked the open concept. I like that I wouldn't have to leave Louis, my doorman, and the one constant in my life, who sends me off with a warm smile almost every day.

"Can we give you a call tomorrow?" I said to Sarah.

"Yes, if anyone else is interested or puts a bid in, I'll call you."

"Thank you," I said, shaking Sarah's hand before leaving.

We were both hungry by the time we were finished. We found a café on Tenth Avenue with a Spanish flair that featured mosaic tiles on the walls. There were light blue cotton tablecloths and white cloth napkins on the tables. After ordering a pitcher of Sangria, I asked Jesse what he was thinking.

"I liked the apartment in your building, and it would certainly be easier to move only one flight up. What do you think?"

"I love my building. After selling my apartment, we should easily be able to get a mortgage for the balance. Having a steady income is beneficial, especially since my income tends to fluctuate. We'll need your employment history to present to the bank. Are you sure this is what you want to do?" I said apprehensively.

"Are you trying to wriggle out on me?"

"I just want you to be certain you know what you're getting yourself into."

"Even if I don't, you'll keep reminding me," Jesse said playfully.

"Compared to me you're practically a saint."

"That's definitely something we can both agree on."

"Very funny," I said, punching Jesse lightly on the arm. "So I guess we're putting an offer in?" I said as enthusiastically as I could muster.

CHAPTER 7

After Jesse left in the morning, I called Sarah and left a message for her. Jesse and I had agreed on the bid we were going to put in. Though it was quite a bit less than the asking price, I knew it was a relocate situation and thought they wouldn't balk at the offer.

I walked the fifteen blocks to my office and called Annie as soon as I got in.

"What's the matter?" she said as soon as she heard the anxiety in my voice.

"I think I made a terrible mistake, and I don't know what to do."

"I have a client coming in for a consultation in five minutes. Can it wait till later? I can meet you at The Dead Poet at 5:30 p.m."

"I'll see you then." Annie is my best friend, my only friend. We met in school when we were thirteen, not too long after my parents died.

I made a pot of coffee and sat down at my desk. For a moment I stared at the photo of my five-year-old self with my parents looking down and smiling at me. Though I'm not sentimental, I like having them close.

***

Annie was already seated at a table for two when I got to The Dead Poet. This is our go-to place for drinks and hors d'oeuvres. The atmosphere is lively, and the décor is a celebration of the lives of writers and poets, with their portraits hung on the mahogany-paneled walls.

"Sit," Annie said. "I already ordered you a glass of wine." Annie is about 100 pounds and maybe 5 feet 2 inches tall on a good day, but can eat more in one sitting than people twice her size. I have no idea where she puts it, and I'm pretty sure she has never worked out a day in her life.

"Thanks." As soon as the wine came, I took a big gulp before the glass even touched the table.

"Tell me what's going on cause you're scaring me a little bit."

"I'm not sure about moving in with Jesse. We went looking at apartments yesterday and all my fears and anxieties came rushing back. I don't know what I was thinking when I told him I would move in with him."

"You were thinking that you loved him and that you wouldn't let fear stop you."

"I don't think I can do it."

"Okay. Let's take it one thought at a time. What exactly are you afraid is going to happen?"

"I'll wind up hating him, or worse, he'll wind up hating me. I won't be able to breathe with him always there."

"I felt the same way before Doug and I started living together. I expected things to change between us but they didn't. When Doug wants to play handball after work or go out for a drink with his friends, he does so, just like when I tell him I'm meeting you. That's why it works. Just because you're married doesn't mean you're joined at the hip twenty-four seven."

"I know that intellectually, but…"

"Without the bullshit, tell me what really worries you?"

"It's not Jesse. I do love him, but I like the way our arrangement is now, seeing each other on the weekends and being by myself during the week. I just don't know if I'm ready to take that next step."

"I want you to be happy, but if you feel that moving in with Jesse isn't the right step for you at this moment, you need to understand that he might choose to walk away from the relationship. Are you prepared to accept that?"

"On the bright side, I have a new case," I said, wanting to change the subject. I went on to explain what I had found out so far.

"I'll play along for the moment. It could be she wanted to be alone for a few days, but from what you're telling me, it sounds as if there's more to it. Switching back to our prior conversation, do you intend to talk to your therapist about the situation with Jesse?"

"No. It's my decision."

"Just promise me you'll think about it some more before you make any rash decisions."

"I will."

***

As I was leaving to go to the office the following morning, my phone rang.

"Ms. Landon, it's Sarah. I just got off the phone with a woman who has agreed to pay the asking price. Unless you're willing to go a little higher than their bid, she and her husband would most likely get the apartment. You'll have to let me know within the next few hours what you decide."

I had mixed emotions when I hung up the phone. Though this would clearly give me a way out, at least for the time being, if I was going to move in with Jesse, I wanted that apartment. What if Jesse said he'd be willing to put in a higher bid, then what? I had no choice but to tell him what the realtor said. I couldn't lie to him.

"Hey, babe," he said, when he answered the phone. "Any news?" He sounded excited.

"I just got a call from Sarah and someone put in a full offer. Unless we go higher, we won't get the apartment."

"What do you think?"

"It's a lot of money. Maybe we shouldn't rush into it. There'll be other places."

"Yeah, but I thought you wanted to stay in your building."

"I do, but the asking price was high to begin with. Something else might show up," I said, trying to sound upbeat.

"Listen, I was actually going to call you. I just spoke to my boss and I have to fly out to Chicago tomorrow. We have a client who was arrested for murder. It seems that he and his partner were mixed up in some shady deals, and without going into too much detail, our client was found at the murder scene of someone he was trying to scam. Our client's partner is gone and we need to find him."

"Why Chicago?"

"Our client thinks his partner has connections there and that's where he's originally from. It may be a wild-goose chase, but that's the best info we have at the moment."

"Does he think his partner killed him?"

"I don't know, but he swears someone is framing him."

"Do you know how long you'll be there?"

"As long as it takes to find him or I'm convinced he's not in Chicago."

"And what will you do if you find him? Do you think he'll come back with you if you ask politely?"

"Wiseass. I have no idea. If I can question him, maybe I can at least find out why he left his partner hanging. I wish there was time to see you before I leave, but my boss wants me on the plane ASAP."

"What do you want to do about the apartment?"

"I guess we can wait; we'll figure it out when I get back. I'll call you from the hotel tomorrow. I love you."

"Love you too."

Part of me was relieved that we weren't going to buy the apartment. I knew I would have to make a decision sooner or later, but for now I was off the hook. Maybe by the time Jesse got back I'd feel differently. Wishful thinking.

CHAPTER 8

I picked up the phone and dialed the number I had for Gail Davis, Katie Lewis's friend. It went straight to voicemail where I left a message. I still knew very little about Katie. Her parents didn't seem to have much to say, and I got the feeling they weren't telling me everything they knew about their daughter. The only piece of information I obtained was from Katie's husband—that she went out at night without telling him where she was going. Though he thought maybe she was meeting a friend, he had no idea if that was the case. The affair angle seemed more plausible to me, but that didn't explain what was going on now and why she disappeared.

My phone was ringing. "Ms. Landon, this is Gail Davis returning your call."

"Thank you. As I mentioned on the phone, I'm a private investigator hired by Katie's parents to find out what, if anything, has happened to her. Would it be possible to meet later?"

"Is downtown okay? There's a coffee bar a few blocks from my apartment. I can text you the name and address."

"No problem. I'll see you then."

No sooner had I hung up than I heard my front door open. When I went into the reception area, Mr. Peterson was standing there.

"What are you doing here?" I said, surprised to see him.

"Can I talk with you?"

"Of course. Let's go into my office. Can I get you any coffee or water?" I said as I nodded for Mr. Peterson to sit.

"No, I'm fine." Mr. Peterson was dressed in business attire: dark blue suit, white shirt, and a gray and blue tie. His full head of dark brown hair was neatly combed and parted on the right side.

"I wasn't expecting you. What's going on?"

"I didn't want to bring this up in front of my wife," he said, shifting in his seat. I waited for him to continue.

"My wife and daughter have a strained relationship. Ever since Katie was a teenager they've butted heads. I was usually the one Katie went to when she was having any problems, and that's why I was surprised to hear the voice message she left for my wife. I would have thought she would have called me. I just find that odd."

"Do you have any idea what was going on with your daughter or why she would just leave abruptly?"

"It's not like her. At first I thought she was angry at my wife and that's why Katie hadn't been returning her calls. Katie can be dramatic. To be honest, I didn't think much of the message she left. I thought she was trying to upset her mother. You see, my wife hasn't been very supportive of Katie's decision to leave her husband. She's kind of old-school. You tough things out."

"Did Katie say anything that would lead you to believe she was in trouble?"

"I would remember something like that," he said, averting my eyes.

"If you know anything else, I need to know."

"I've told you everything."

"Well, thank you for coming in."

When he left, I wondered why he felt the need to come all the way to my office to tell me that his wife and daughter were not on good terms. I was also curious whether he was jealous that Katie had called his wife and not him, or maybe he was angry at his wife for not picking up when Katie called. Detective Marks was right when he said family dynamics could be complicated.

CHAPTER 9

Gail Davis was absolutely stunning as I watched her walk into the coffee bar in her East Village neighborhood. Her tight jeans fit her long, lanky legs to perfection. She had on an oversized white sweater and black leather boots that came just below her knees. She tucked one side of her long, straight blonde hair behind her ear. When she got closer to me, I noticed she had a scar that ran about two inches down the right side of her face.

"Thank you for meeting me," I said.

We ordered coffee from the barista and sat down at a round marbled table for two.

"Of course. To tell you the truth, I was getting worried when the last few times I called Katie, she hadn't called me back. It wasn't like her not to return my calls. Her mother contacted me about the message she left and asked if I knew where Katie was."

"Why don't you tell me about Katie. I didn't get the feeling that her parents were very forthcoming when I spoke to them." Gail didn't seem at all surprised at my remark.

"Katie and I met in college where we were roommates and became best friends. She never looked at me the way most people did when they first saw me. I used to be extremely self-conscious. Now I sometimes forget it's there," she said, lightly touching her cheek.

"May I ask how it happened?"

"When I was five years old, a disturbed boy from my block, who was about twelve, thought it would be fun to slash my face with a switchblade. I underwent plastic surgery when I was older, so it looks a lot better now. Anyway, I'm assuming you want to know what was going on with Katie. The truth is, I'm not sure. I know she didn't want to be married anymore."

"Do you know what prompted that?"

"She met Paul right after college, and they dated for a few months before getting married. I believe she thought she was in love with him, but I wasn't entirely convinced. It turns out that Paul was very possessive; he would become jealous if another guy even glanced at Katie. She felt trapped, believing that Paul was suffocating her."

"Is that why she started going out at night?"

"Yes. She didn't want to hurt Paul, but being with him was getting to be too difficult. At some point she asked him for a divorce."

"How did he take it?"

"He was furious. He stalked her and called her at all hours. Sometimes he would show up at her place begging her to let him in."

"I spoke with Paul and he told me that Katie wanted to start a family right away, but he didn't."

"Katie never mentioned that to me. Why would Katie want to start a family when she was trying to get away from him? That doesn't make sense."

Was Paul lying? Maybe he didn't want to share with me the fact that he was possessive of Katie.

"Do you think he could have something to do with her disappearance?" I said.

"I can't imagine."

"Why do you say that?"

"Paul doesn't strike me as a killer. Besides, he loved her."

I didn't agree with Gail. When pushed, people are capable of anything. If Paul was as jealous as Gail said, and Katie was rebuffing him, he might have lost it.

"Do you know if he was physically abusive?"

"I can't be certain, though I didn't see any signs that Paul hurt her."

"Do you know where Katie went at night?"

Gail didn't answer right away. She looked off into the distance. I wondered if she knew but was debating whether to tell me.

"She was having an affair," Gail said, as she reached for her coffee. "We were together one evening at a restaurant, sitting at the bar, when this guy started talking to Katie. We joined him and his friend at a table where we spent a few hours together. I could tell Katie was attracted to Peter. He seemed like a nice person. She didn't find out until she had been with him a few times that he was married. By that point, I think she was hooked. I told her I didn't think it was a good idea to get involved with him, but she had no intention of listening to me."

"Do you know his last name?"

"Crawford, Peter Crawford. She never talked about him. She knew I wasn't happy about the fact that he was married."

"Would she have gone away with him and not told anyone?"

"I doubt it. Besides, she never would have left her students. She loves being a teacher."

"Do you know where they would meet?"

"I don't, though I doubt it was at her place because she couldn't trust that Paul wouldn't show up unexpectedly."

"During the conversation, did Mr. Crawford mention where he worked or lived?"

"I believe he worked in a tech job, but other than that, I don't know anything else about him. I would guess he might live in Manhattan, but that would just be a guess. He could live in the suburbs for all I know."

"How old would you say he is?"

"Probably in his thirties, maybe late thirties."

"Is there anything else you can remember about him?"

"Besides being very handsome, I don't think so."

"What about the other guy who was there?"

"I couldn't tell you anything about him. I only got his first name, Brian."

"Can you think of any place Katie may have gone?"

"I can't. I'm sorry. Do you think something has happened to her?"

"I have no reason to believe that at the moment. Here's my card if you think of anything else. By the way, you mentioned you weren't sure if Katie was in love with her husband when she married him. Why is that?"

"This is just a guess, but I believe deep down Katie sensed something was off with Paul. You know when someone's in love, how happy they are, yet I never felt that from her. Katie and her mother were constantly at odds, like oil and water. Perhaps she saw marriage as a way out of the turmoil in her house. One other thing. Something was definitely bothering Katie, but whatever it was, she never told me."

"How do you know that?"

"She was my best friend. I just knew."

I didn't doubt what Gail said. I always knew when something was off with Annie.

"One last question. Do you know if Peter Crawford was the only guy Katie picked up at a bar?"

"I'm pretty sure. I was usually with her when we went out."

"But you're not a hundred percent?"

"No," she said, looking uncertain.

"If you think of anything else, please call me."

I grabbed a taxi back to my apartment. What Gail said was very interesting. I think we do tend to ignore our inner voice when it might get in the way of our goal. It also corroborated what Mr. Peterson told me about his daughter's relationship with her mother. So why would she call her mother and not her father?

I was eager to find Peter Crawford. Could he have something to do with Katie's disappearance? And did Katie's husband know about her affair?

CHAPTER 10

As I was heating leftover Chinese food from two days ago, I turned on my laptop in search of Peter Crawford. How many Peter Crawfords could there be? As it turned out there were a few, but only one who was in his thirties. He lived in Greenwich, Connecticut.

I went into my databases and pulled up the report I found on Mr. Crawford. He was thirty-seven. There was an Amy Crawford listed, age thirty-two. I was guessing it was his wife. No children were mentioned, and it didn't list a place of employment. If he did work in technology, it's possible that he was freelancing or maybe he lied to Katie about what he did. I spat out the report and copied down his address in Connecticut. I then emailed the company I use to obtain cell phone records, requesting Katie's records from the last two months because I was curious about who she had been in contact with recently. I also requested Katie's last month's credit card statement.

* * *

The following morning I went for a run in the park that's conveniently only a few blocks from my apartment. I usually run about three or four times a week, early in the morning when there's fewer people around. The park has its share of runners, and in the late morning, the nannies come with their charges to enjoy the playground that's equipped with slides, climbers, swings, and seesaws.

When I got back, I showered, dressed, and turned on the coffee maker. While the coffee was dripping, I decided to take a run up to Connecticut and check out the address I had for Peter Crawford. This could be a wild-goose chase since I wasn't even sure it was the same Peter Crawford Katie was seeing.

Two hours later, I was turning onto a tree-lined street in Greenwich, Connecticut. Each of the houses was on at least a half-acre of property and set back from the street with pristine manicured lawns. The house was a white center hall colonial with a black-painted wooden door, similar to the other houses in the area. Greenwich is a very affluent town, with many residents commuting into New York City for their jobs on Wall Street.

I waited in my car for a few minutes before walking up to the front door. I knocked and then rang the doorbell. I was pretty sure the woman who was standing in front of me was Peter Crawford's wife, Amy. I was surprised at the way she looked, her blonde hair stringy as if it hadn't been washed in days. She wore a torn sweatshirt and faded jeans, and her eyes were bloodshot.

"Can I help you?" she asked, her voice barely above a whisper.

"I'm looking for Peter Crawford." The moment I said his name, she flinched as if I had struck her.

"Why?" Her eyes looked away, filled with sadness.

"He was a witness to an automobile accident." I hesitated, knowing I had no reason to upset her further by revealing the truth.

"Peter's dead," she said, her voice trembling. The weight of her words hit me like a punch to the gut.

"I'm so sorry. What happened?" I asked, genuinely concerned.

"Who are you?" she replied, her gaze filled with suspicion.

"My name's Maddie Landon. I'm a private investigator," I replied, handing her my card.

"Why are you here?" she said with a confused look on her face.

"I'm investigating an automobile accident that your husband witnessed. I wanted to ask him a few questions."

"He was murdered."

I was momentarily speechless, the gravity of what she said sinking in.

"Do the police know who did it?" I managed to ask, my mind racing with a million questions.

"No. I need to get back in the house," she said, stepping back.

I didn't want her to go. "Can I just ask you where he was found?"

"Please leave," she said, her voice firm, and with that the door closed, leaving me standing, trying to make sense of what I had just been told.

I walked to my car and turned on the engine, but didn't leave. If Katie Lewis was involved with Peter Crawford, did she have any connection to his death?

Driving back, I remembered that I had no idea if the Peter Crawford who was killed was the same person Katie was having an affair with. First, I had to find out if I had the right person.

When I got to my office, I looked up the number I had for one of my contacts from my days with the New York

City Police Department. Though it was Saturday, I was hoping he would be on duty.

"Seth, it's Maddie Landon. Please call me back when you get this message."

I drank two cups of coffee while I was waiting for Seth to call me back. I picked up as soon as I heard the phone ring.

"Hey, Maddie, great to hear from you, though I'm guessing this isn't a social call."

Seth was one of the guys I was friendly with in my squad. He was one of the few people I got along with who didn't think he was full of himself. I never got the impression that I was a favorite in my precinct.

"You're right, but it's nice to hear your voice."

"What's going on?"

I explained the situation and what I needed from him. "Do you think you can get the information? Unfortunately, I don't have much to go on except a name and address. I have no idea when or where he was murdered. I need a photo if you can get one."

"I'll get back to you as soon as I have something."

Until Seth called me back, there wasn't much I could do. If it was the same guy, that changed everything.

I poured my third cup of coffee and started searching for any articles related to Peter Crawford's death. I found a small article that just said that the body of a local resident of Greenwich, Connecticut, Peter Crawford, was found murdered from blunt force trauma to the head last Thursday evening. It didn't give any other details. That was over a week ago.

I kept looking for other articles, but there were none. I heard my phone vibrating from inside my pocket.

"How's the Windy City?" I said to Jesse when I saw it was him.

"Colder than New York," Jesse said.

"How's the hotel?"

"It's a Hampton Inn, not too shabby. There's an outdoor pool, but unless I'm in the mood to freeze my ass off, I think I'll stick to dry land. The hotel offers a limited buffet breakfast, which suits me just fine."

"Any luck so far?"

"Not yet. I'm just getting my bearings and making some contacts. The guy has a sister and a mother living in Chicago. I might start with them. Do you miss me?"

"Nah! I've been too busy painting the town red."

"Pretty fast work considering I've only been gone a day."

"You know me," I said, chuckling.

"That's what worries me. Trouble seems to find you."

"Speaking of trouble." I caught Jesse up to speed on my case.

"So you think your subject is somehow involved?"

"I have no idea."

"Have you thought of the possibility she might be dead?" Jesse said.

"It crossed my mind, but I'm keeping my fingers crossed that's not the case. Right now I'm waiting on my contact to hopefully get a photo of the guy to confirm whether he's the person she was having the affair with."

"Keep me posted. I love you."

"Me too. Sleep well."

***

The alarm woke me up at 7:00 a.m. Sunday felt different without Jesse. It's rare that we spend a weekend apart. Though it was warm and cozy under the covers, I knew I intended to spend the day working.

As I was getting dressed, I heard a ding from my phone. It was an email with an attachment from Seth. I quickly opened up my computer, downloaded the attachment and printed out the pages from my copier, my pulse beating a little faster.

CHAPTER 11

Seth was able to obtain a copy of the preliminary police report and a photo of Peter Crawford. I could feel my excitement growing. These are the moments that get my juices going. Jesse is not wrong when he says I get a rush when I'm working a case; my anxiety level also goes up a few notches.

The first thing I did was to send the photo to Gail Davis, keeping my fingers crossed this was the same person Katie Lewis was having the affair with. I warned her that it might be hard to look at. According to the police report, Peter Crawford was found murdered at the Horizon Motel in Yonkers from several blows to the back of the head. There was no one else found in the room with him and they hadn't identified the weapon used. There was no forced entry and no witnesses. A cleaning lady had found the victim. I know how hard it is getting any forensic evidence from a motel room with a million prints all over the place.

A minute later, Gail Davis called me.

"Oh my God, it's him. What happened?"

"The police don't know. I would delete the photo."

"What about Katie?" I could hear the fear in her voice.

"Listen, Gail. We have no reason to believe that anything has happened to her."

"Her phone is dead. I can't leave her a message."

"That doesn't mean anything," was all I could think of saying to keep Gail calm. Did Katie leave in a hurry because she witnessed what happened or did she have something to do with Crawford's murder?

"I will let you know as soon as I find out anything. In the meantime, please keep this to yourself and don't say anything to her parents. You'll only worry them."

When we hung up, I read over the police report again. Since this was only a preliminary report, it didn't go into too many details. I'm sure the police were checking his cell phone records. If Katie's number popped up, they'd be looking to question her.

I left my apartment and drove up to the Horizon Motel located off the Saw Mill River Parkway in the City of Yonkers in lower Westchester County. Though Yonkers is considered middle class, like a lot of cities, they have their share of seedy areas. The motel was one step up from a Motel 6. There was no pool or trees outside, just a long row of motel rooms. I parked in front of the motel office.

"Excuse me," I said to the grubby-looking guy behind the desk. He looked to be in his thirties, skinny, and sporting a goatee, with glazed-over eyes. If it was a scene in a movie, you might be wondering if he had rigged up a camera to spy in the rooms.

"I was hoping you could help me out. I'm a private investigator looking into the death of a guy by the name of Peter Crawford, the man who was found murdered in one of your motel rooms."

His eyes opened wide. "Uh! Can I see some identification?" I showed him my card. "What do you want to know?"

I pulled up the photo of Katie Lewis that was on my phone. "Can you tell me if you've seen this woman?"

"I'm not sure if I'm allowed to share that information."

I could see he was wavering, but I knew his type. He would spill his guts if I showed him a little attention. "I promise I won't tell anyone," I said, giving him my sexiest smile.

"Maybe," he said with a smirk on his face. "She may have been with him, but the woman never came inside. She stayed in the car while he registered."

"Were you on duty the day he was killed?"

"Hmm. I'm not sure."

I knew he was being coy. "Would this help your memory?" I said, handing him a twenty.

"It helps a little." I reluctantly gave him another twenty.

"It was around 7:00 p.m. when he came in for a room. Like I said, there was a woman in the car, but I didn't get a good look at her. The room I gave him was down at the very end, so I didn't hear anything."

"Was he ever here before?"

"He didn't look familiar."

"Who found him?"

"The cleaning lady the next day."

"Was the room next to him occupied?"

"Yeah, but I can't give you that information."

"What about outside cameras?"

"Are you kidding. The owner doesn't want cameras and I don't think any of the people staying here want them either."

So I was back to square one. Unless he was seeing someone else, Katie Lewis was probably in the room with Crawford the night he died.

"Was his car here in the morning?"

"It was, but I wasn't on duty when the police came."

If his car was here, how did Katie get back? And when she got back, where was she going in such a hurry?

CHAPTER 12

I was curious if the police had questioned the people staying in the room next to Crawford's.

"I didn't get your name," I said to the clerk.

"Marty."

"Listen, Marty. The woman who was with Crawford that night disappeared. Her parents are worried sick. They don't know if their daughter is dead. You could really help me out if I knew the name of the person who was in the adjacent room."

"I could get into big trouble if I gave you that name."

"What can I offer you to make it worth your while?"

"How about if we go in the back room. There's a nice couch in there."

"I'd love to take you up on your offer, but my boyfriend has a mean temper, and if he ever found out, he'd come and beat the shit out of you. I wouldn't want that to happen," I said with a straight face.

"He doesn't have to know. It'll be our little secret," he said with a mischievous gaze.

"As tempting as that sounds, no can do. Is there anything else?"

"How about you open up a couple of those buttons on your shirt."

"Let me see the name first."

Marty opened the register book to the day Peter Crawford checked in. "Here it is. His name is Robert Towland."

"Let me see," I said, quickly moving the book closer to me.

"Okay, now it's your turn. Start opening your shirt so I can get a look at those sweet tits."

His repulsiveness made my skin crawl. I was so angry I shoved the book hard and it landed on the floor behind the counter.

"What the fuck," he said, as he reached down to retrieve it. I ran out the door, into my car, and drove around to the side of the motel. I could hear him yelling and cursing as I was fleeing.

This guy was an idiot if he actually thought I was going to give him a show. I parked my car at the far end of the parking lot where I had a clear view if any of the cleaning people were working. I had no clue when they made their rounds, but I thought I would stick around just in case. As I waited, I wondered why Peter Crawford, who obviously had money, would wind up at a shitty place like this. Maybe it was the thrill of it or a safe, out-of-the-way place he wouldn't be seen.

I turned on the radio, listening to a John Denver song: "Rocky Mountain High." Though he was more my parents' generation, Annie is a big fan of his music. When he died in a plane crash while piloting his own plane, I had to console her for days.

I was nodding off when I heard a police siren from the road whizzing by. When I jerked up, I saw a woman with a cleaning cart going into one of the rooms. I quickly walked over, hoping she was the one who had found Peter's body.

"Excuse me, my name's Maddie. I hope I didn't startle you."

"No, I was just going in to clean the room," she said in broken English

"I was wondering if you could help me. I'm investigating the death of a man found in Room 108. Were you the one who found him?" Her name tag on her uniform said Maria. She was short and on the chunky side. Maria had a net over her dark-colored hair and wore yellow latex gloves on her hands.

"Please, I don't want any trouble."

"I promise you I'm not here to cause you any problems. I just want to ask you a few questions. It must have been horrible to find this person dead."

"I started screaming. I was so scared. His face was like a ghost and there was a big dark stain on the floor near his head." She made the sign of the cross.

"Did you go into the room?"

"No! No! As soon as I saw him lying on the floor I ran." I knew from experience that sometimes people don't want to admit that they may linger a few seconds.

"Are you sure? Maybe before you ran off you saw something or you took a closer peek."

"His shirt was off. That's all I remember," she said quickly.

"Maria, if there is anything else, please tell me."

"His buckle and zipper were undone," she said, averting my eyes.

"Good. Is there anything else that caught your attention?"

"Please, I know nothing else."

"Okay, thank you, Maria. Here's my card if you recall anything more."

Where was Katie Lewis when Peter Crawford was killed? Was she hiding somewhere? Did she see who the killer was or did she kill Crawford? Too many unanswered questions.

CHAPTER 13

I stopped at the deli before heading back to my office and brought back a tuna fish sandwich on a hard roll. While taking a bite of my sandwich, I searched the name Robert Towland in my databases. It appeared from the report that he was married. If he wasn't at the motel with his wife, would he be reluctant to talk to me? It listed that he was an attorney on Main Street in White Plains, though it was unclear from the report whether he was a sole practitioner or worked at a firm. Unfortunately, Mr. Towland would have to wait till business hours tomorrow morning.

***

First thing in the morning, I entered Mr. Towland's business address in my GPS and headed to his office in White Plains, a city in Westchester County with a fairly large downtown business district with restaurants, coffee shops, and parks. Once I was on Main Street, I found metered parking about a block from Towland's building.

"Hey, Annie," I said when I saw it was her calling.

"What are you up to?" she said.

"I've been working on the investigation I told you about. Oh, and Jesse's in Chicago trying to track down some guy on a murder case."

"For how long?"

"He's not sure. Could be a while, depending if or when he can locate the person."

"Why don't we catch up. I'll meet you at our place tomorrow for breakfast at eight o'clock."

The six-story building was primarily occupied by attorneys. After walking up three flights, I found my way to Robert Towland's office door, which was etched with his title as a real estate attorney.

The woman behind the desk looked up as I entered the room. She was rather young; pretty with a fair complexion. Her nails were painted bright red, as were her lips.

"Can I help you?"

"Is Mr. Towland in?"

"Do you have an appointment?"

"No, it's a personal matter," I said, handing her my card.

After looking at it for several seconds, she got up and walked into his office. What are the chances Towland was at the motel with his receptionist?

When she came out, she said he would be with me in a few minutes. It gave me the opportunity to chat with her.

"Do you mind if I ask you your name?"

"It's Cindy Draper."

"Have you been working here for a while?"

"About a year, but I'm also in college studying business. I've never met a female private investigator. It must be exciting."

"Actually, most of the time it's pretty mundane. How do you like working for Mr. Towland?" I said casually.

"He's nice," she said, as I noticed her blushing a little.

At that point, Robert Towland came out and introduced himself. "Please come in. Why is a private investigator interested in talking with me?" he said, as he motioned me to sit. His office had files strewn everywhere. Maybe he had a system. The beige carpet and matching drapes looked old.

Mr. Towland didn't strike me as a ladies' man, but we know that appearances have nothing to do with cheating. Men and women do it all the time for different reasons. Towland was approximately 5 feet 9 inches tall and had a middle-aged spread. He was in his fifties with a receding hairline.

"There was a man who was killed at the Horizon Motel about ten days ago. I'm looking into the disappearance of a woman who may have been with him at the time he was murdered." Small beads of sweat appeared on his forehead.

"Again, how can I help you?" he said, trying to recover.

"Look, I'm not here to cause you any trouble. What you do is your business, but I know you occupied the adjacent room on the day the guy was killed. I just want to know if you heard or saw anything."

"How did you get my name?"

"That's not important, and like I said, I don't care who you were with. Just tell me what you know and this conversation goes no further. Did you happen to see this woman at the motel?" I said, showing him Katie's photo.

I could see he was reluctant; he didn't want to get involved.

"No."

"Do you remember hearing anything from the room?"

"I only heard voices, but I couldn't tell you if they were male or female. They weren't talking loud and I wasn't there to listen to what was going on in the next room."

"Did you happen to hear any screaming or a loud commotion coming from the room at any time?"

"As I said, I didn't hear anything. I'm sorry. I can't help you. You said the woman is missing?"

"Yes. Nobody has heard from her in the past week or so. One other question. Can you tell me what time you arrived at the motel and what time you left?"

"I'm not exactly sure, maybe around 4:00 p.m. and left around 8:00 p.m."

"If you remember anything at all, you have my number."

If Towland was there from approximately 4:00 to 8:00 p.m. and Peter Crawford didn't check in till after 7:00 p.m., it's possible Towland wasn't there when Crawford was murdered. If it was Katie in the room with Crawford, what the hell happened to her?

CHAPTER 14

When I arrived at my office, I noticed I had an email with an attachment. When I opened it up, I was looking at Katie's cell phone records and her last credit card statement that I had requested. The printer spat out the pages and I started sifting through them. What struck me was how many times her husband had called Katie. There must have been dozens of calls to her. Maybe Katie's friend Gail was right about him. Was he stalking Katie? I made a note to myself to have another chat with him.

There were some calls from Peter Crawford. The last call came in on the morning of the day he was murdered. Were they talking about spending time at the motel? Some of the other calls listed were between her and her friend Gail. There was a number I didn't recognize that was listed several times.

I picked up the phone and dialed that number.

"James Peterson."

"Mr. Peterson," I said. "This is Maddie Landon." I was surprised there were several calls between them. I had gotten the impression they hadn't spoken very often in the last few weeks before she disappeared.

"I'm so glad you called. Do you have any information on Katie? We're so worried."

"When we last spoke, you mentioned that Katie told you her husband had been calling her quite a bit. I was wondering if you could fill me in on your conversations with your daughter."

"I see." Did I hear reluctance in his voice?

"Mr. Peterson, may I remind you that in order for me to do everything possible to locate Katie, I need to know everything that you know."

"I didn't want to say anything in front of my wife. She would only be more upset than she already is. It was more than phone calls. Sometimes he would show up at her place and bang on the door to let him in. I think she was scared of him."

"Why didn't you tell me any of this when you came to my office?"

"Because I didn't believe Paul would actually harm my daughter. I just thought he was angry that she left him, and I didn't want him to get into trouble."

"Is there anything else you could think of even if you feel it's not relevant?" I said, trying to keep my temper in check.

"This is most likely nothing, but Katie told me she was taking tennis lessons."

"You're probably right. Would you happen to know where she took these lessons?"

"I have no idea."

"I need to come by later tonight and tell you what I've found out so far."

"Why can't you tell me now?"

"Because I work for both you and your wife, and she has a right to know what's going on. If 7:00 p.m. works, I'll see you then."

When I hung up, I reached for the credit card statement. There didn't seem to be any unusual charges. Then I saw it, a charge from the Vanderbilt Tennis Club.

That saved me a lot of time tracking down the place where she was taking tennis lessons.

Before leaving the office to confront Paul Lewis at the bank, I went across the hall to see Cousin Will.

"Hi, Mary, how are the kids?"

"They're good. Getting big. Haven't seen much of you lately." Mary is Will's indispensable assistant. His insurance agency wouldn't run without her.

"I know. I've been busy."

"Let me guess, another case."

"You are a mind reader."

"Go ahead in."

"Hey, cuz. You know one day I'm going to catch you doing something besides having your nose stuck in a pile of papers."

"As long as it doesn't include sleeping or picking my nose."

If someone asked me how I would describe Will's dress attire, it would be one word: preppy. Right down to his classic argyle socks. As far as his looks, Will was handsome, clean-cut, with a great smile showing off his white teeth. Will is my cousin on my father's side. After my parents died in the car crash, Will became my protector, being a few years older than me.

"That would be a lot more fun. I'd like a photo of that to send to Sophie."

"Which reminds me, did Sophie call you about Noah's birthday party?" Sophie is Will's wife and Noah is their soon-to-be three-year-old son.

"Yes. I can't believe he's going to be three. Any ideas what I should get him?"

"Surprise us as long as whatever you buy him isn't going to destroy the house."

"By the way, I recently heard from the DA's office, and the guy who tried to kill me on my last case took a deal, so I won't have to testify."

"How do you feel about that?"

"I'm okay with it. Between the rape charge and the attempt on my life, he won't be seeing the light of day anytime soon. Well, off to fight crime."

"Be safe."

"Always." Though we both knew that wasn't exactly true.

CHAPTER 15

I drove up to Riverdale to confront Paul Lewis. I knew showing up at his place of business without warning was going to tick him off, but I didn't like being lied to.

When he saw me walk in, his eyebrows shot up. "What are you doing here?" he said in a whisper, quickly closing his office door as we entered. His small office included a desk with the usual electronics and a comfortable-looking chair. I noticed he had a photo of Katie on the side of his desk.

"Why did you lie to me?"

"What are you talking about?"

"Apparently, you conveniently forgot to tell me that you were stalking your wife."

"You have no right to come to my workplace."

"Well, then you should have told me the truth from the beginning."

"I don't know who's been filling your head with lies," he said, turning away from me. "I'm sorry. I should have told you, but I wouldn't use the word stalking. I just wanted to see her, and I was afraid you might think I had something to do with her disappearance," he said, when he finally turned and looked at me.

"Didn't you think I would have found out eventually?"

"I guess I wasn't thinking clearly. All I wanted was to get Katie to pay attention to me. I knew we could work things out if she would only listen to what I had to say."

He really believed that's all it would take to get his wife back.

"I have no idea where Katie is. I'm just as upset as her parents are."

"Did you know that Katie was having an affair?"

"I had my suspicions, but I didn't know for sure." I couldn't tell if he was lying or he really didn't know, and decided not to mention the fact that the person she was having the affair with was dead.

"Do you have any idea where Katie would go if she needed a place to stay or hide?"

"No. And why would she need a place to hide?"

"I'm just asking. Is there anything else you'd like to tell me?"

"Just find my wife."

***

Later that evening I pulled up to the Petersons' house. When Mrs. Peterson opened the door, I noticed a slight tic in her left eye. She rushed me into the living room, and we all sat in the same seats as we did when I was last here. Mrs. Peterson's hands were twisting as she waited for me to speak. I wasn't sure how much I should divulge, but decided to tell them only what they needed to know at this point.

"First, I want you to know I have no reason to believe anything has happened to your daughter, but there are some things I found out. It appears that your son-in-law has been harassing Katie. He's been calling her several times a day and showing up unannounced at her place."

"Why didn't she tell me?" Mrs. Peterson said, close to tears.

"I don't know. Maybe she didn't want to worry you," I said.

"Did you know what was going on with our daughter?" Mrs. Peterson said, with an angry look in her eyes.

"I'm sorry, I didn't want to upset you," Mr. Peterson said, refusing to meet her eyes.

"Do you think he harmed Katie?" he said to me.

"As I said, I have no reason to believe anything has happened to your daughter. What I did find out was that she was seeing someone." The Petersons looked at each other, both seemingly surprised at what I had just told them.

"Have you questioned this person yet? He might know what happened to Katie," Mrs. Peterson said, her eyes filled with hope.

I was debating what to say next.

"I was recently informed that the person your daughter was having an affair with has died." I wasn't prepared to tell them he was murdered.

"Oh my God!" Mrs. Peterson's eyes widened.

"How did he die?" Mr. Peterson asked.

"I don't know. I believe his death is being investigated."

I decided not to go into where he died or that Katie might have been with Peter Crawford at the time of his death. They didn't have to know those details at the moment, and I certainly didn't want the police to find out if Katie was with him.

"But if she's missing, wouldn't it be related to his death?" Mr. Peterson said.

"It could just be a coincidence. It's possible that Katie needed to get away because her husband was harassing her." It did sound pretty lame, but telling them what I really thought, until I knew more, might be too much for them to handle.

"I just don't understand any of this. Why would my daughter have an affair? I didn't raise her to cheat on her husband."

"Please, Dorothy, don't be so hard on her. She wasn't with Paul anymore," Mr. Peterson said, trying to calm his wife.

"If something has happened to Katie, the police would have notified you. Please keep that in mind."

"So now what?" Mr. Peterson said.

"I'm going on the assumption your daughter may have left on her own for whatever reason. I'm running down all leads. As soon as I have any more information, I will let you know. Until that time, we have to assume Katie is safe."

I was just as baffled as the Petersons as to what happened to their daughter. Did she kill Peter Crawford in the heat of passion or did she see who did it and was in hiding? The chilling thought that crossed my mind was that she might be dead and her body hadn't been found yet. I was hoping I was wrong.

CHAPTER 16

In the morning, I was sitting at a table for two in the French Café. As soon as you stepped inside, the irresistible aroma of the buttery pastries filled the air, making your mouth water in anticipation of one of their delicious croissants. While I waited for Annie, I ordered a cup of coffee. Although I'd never been to France, the posters adorning the walls—featuring iconic sights like the Eiffel Tower and the French Riviera—had me wondering if I'd get the chance to visit there someday. My thoughts drifted back to the present as I saw Annie walk in.

"Hi, sweetie," Annie said, giving me a kiss on my cheek before she sat down. "That coffee smells wonderful. I'm starving." Annie was dressed for success in a striped blue suit with a pink silk blouse. Her beautiful short brown curls looked great framed against her oval face. I, on the other hand, was in my usual work attire.

When the waitress came over, we both ordered pancakes with blueberries and bacon crisp.

"How's business?" I asked after the waitress left.

"Pretty good. We got a few new clients in the past couple of weeks." Annie is a matrimonial attorney who entered into a partnership over a year ago with another attorney.

"I'm hoping we can afford to hire an associate within the next couple of months."

"That's great. Now maybe you and Doug can work on having my godchild."

"You're hysterical."

Annie had miscarried after being involved in an automobile accident. For a long time she was scared to get pregnant again. Now that she and Doug were trying, I knew Annie was relieved knowing if she took time off, Matt, her partner, would have help with the workload.

"So tell me, what's going on with your case?"

"I wish I knew." I went on to tell Annie everything I had discovered so far. "There are a couple of scenarios to consider: First, if Katie was in that motel room with Peter Crawford, it's possible she killed him—perhaps it was an accident during a lovers' quarrel, and in her panic, she fled the scene. Alternatively, she might have witnessed the crime and is now on the run. In either case, she returned to her apartment and left in a hurry. This raises an important question: If she didn't commit the crime, then who did? And why wouldn't she go to the police?"

"There is another possibility; have you considered that she may be dead? And if she is, then who was the person in her apartment?" Annie said.

"Then why wasn't her body found? More to the point, why would the murderer take her from the motel room and kill her somewhere else? But if she did get away, then we're back to the question, why didn't she go to the police?"

"Maybe she saw the killer and was frightened to get the police involved for whatever reason," Annie said.

"Possibly. So besides Katie, who else had a motive to kill Peter Crawford? Could it have something to do with his work or maybe it was Crawford's wife? If the wife knew he was cheating, could she have killed him or hired someone to do it? I guess it's too early to make any assumptions," I said.

"Where do you go from here?"

"Your guess is as good as mine."

***

When I got to the office, I took out Katie's cell phone records. I wanted to take another glance in case I missed something. Between the last two months' statements, there were several pages of phone calls. I looked at each page carefully when I noticed there was another number that I had overlooked.

It turned out to be a disconnected number, which likely indicated it was from an untraceable burner phone. I sent the number to a specialist who traces phone numbers, but if he couldn't find anything, I doubted anyone I have access to would know more about it.

I was pouring myself a cup of coffee when I remembered something Mr. Peterson had told me when we spoke; he mentioned that Katie was taking tennis lessons. Though I doubted it was important, I still needed to check it out. I heard my phone ringing; it was Gail Davis.

"Ms. Landon, I was calling to see if you found out anything more about Katie. I can't stop thinking about her, and her phone is still dead."

"At this point I'm tracking down all leads. As I told her parents, we have to assume Katie is alive unless I hear anything to the contrary. Her father told me that Katie was taking tennis lessons. Did she say anything to you?"

"She did. I suppose I didn't consider it important enough to mention."

"It may not be, but it doesn't hurt to look into it."

"Do the police know who killed Peter Crawford?" Gail said.

"They're still investigating. Can you tell me if there were any problems between Katie and Peter that you were aware of?"

"Are you thinking that Katie killed Peter?" Gail said, with alarm in her voice.

"If there were any problems, I'd like to know."

"Katie didn't care if Peter was married since she was still married herself. She did tell me that the sex was really great, and I'm pretty sure she wasn't looking for anything more at the moment. I hope that answers your question."

"Thank you, Gail. If you think of anything else, please call me."

As soon as I got off the phone, I looked up the Vanderbilt Tennis Club in Grand Central Station. According to what I read, they had both adult group clinics as well as private lessons. I wrote down the number.

After thinking about it, I was fairly certain they wouldn't disclose any information over the phone about individuals registered for their classes. I called an Uber and waited outside.

CHAPTER 17

I found my way to the fourth floor of the Vanderbilt Building, which connects directly to Grand Central Station. Grand Central Station was officially opened in February of 1913. In 1975, it was scheduled for demolition until Jackie Kennedy Onassis joined with the Municipal Arts Society to save the terminal. They won, and the historic railway station was designated a New York City landmark. The main concourse is the center of the terminal. If you look up, you'll see a vaulted plastic ceiling with a celestial mural depicting the zodiac constellations and thousands of stars against a turquoise background, creating a stunning starry night effect. The station has a variety of stores and food vendors, including some upscale restaurants and bars and a wonderful gourmet food market where you can buy everything from meats to vegetables to cheeses.

The Vanderbilt Tennis Club had one regulation-size indoor hard court, two automated practice courts, and a fully equipped fitness room. Considering how upscale the place was, I questioned how Katie could afford the lessons on her salary. Maybe Peter Crawford was helping her with the payments.

"Excuse me," I said to the young, perky-looking woman dressed in a white tennis outfit and her blonde hair pulled up in a ponytail. "Do you work here?" I asked her.

There was a tennis clinic going on with five women and one instructor, and the other two courts each had someone practicing with balls coming out of an automated ball machine.

"Yes, my name is Leslie. Are you interested in taking tennis lessons?"

"Not today. My name is Maddie Landon," I said, handing her my card. "I'm working on an investigation involving a missing woman who I believe takes tennis lessons at your facility. Her name is Katie Lewis." A look of surprise crossed her face.

"Why yes, Katie usually comes here later in the day. She's missing? I hope she's alright."

"When was the last time Katie was here?"

"I'd have to look it up. Can you excuse me, I'll be right back." As Leslie walked away, a nice-looking guy around thirty, wearing his tennis whites, came over.

"Hi, my name's Jake. Can I help you?" He seemed pretty friendly.

"Leslie was looking something up for me. Do you know Katie Lewis?"

"Of course; she attends our clinics. Is there a problem?"

"She's missing."

"I don't understand. What do you mean missing?" I felt Jake's blue eyes boring down on me. Just then, Leslie came back.

"The last time she was here was three weeks ago," Leslie said. "Jake, Ms. Landon is a private investigator. Jake's running the clinics that Katie has been attending."

"Did Katie happen to mention she wouldn't be coming here for a while?"

"Not to me," Leslie said. "Did she say anything to you?" she asked, looking at Jake.

"Nothing. Now I'm worried. She's been coming fairly regularly for the past couple of months. She was even thinking of taking some private lessons, but I think money was an issue," Jake said.

"Did she seem upset, or did she say anything to either of you that indicated something was bothering her?"

"Not to me," Jake said.

"I'm not always here when Katie is, but the last time I saw her she seemed fine."

"Is there anything we can do to help?" Jake said.

"Was there anyone here she was friendly with?"

"Not that I know of," Jake said.

"What about Stacey?" Leslie said to Jake.

"I didn't know they were friendly."

"I once saw them leaving together. I thought I overheard something about going for coffee," Leslie said.

"Would it be possible to get her contact information?"

"Sure."

"Are we allowed to give that information out?" Jake said to Leslie, his eyes glaring at her.

Was Jake annoyed that Leslie was giving out personal information?

"I think in this situation it would be fine. I'll get it."

"I always wanted to learn how to play tennis. It must be very challenging, but fun at the same time," I said to Jake.

"I enjoy teaching if that's what you mean," he said in a curt manner.

"Here you go," Leslie said when she returned.

"Thank you, and if you think of anything that might be helpful, please contact me." On the way out, I picked up Jake's card from the desk. I got the feeling that he wasn't particularly happy about Leslie helping me. I wondered what that was about.

***

I took a taxi back to my office and called Stacey Adam.

"Ms. Adam," I said when she answered. "My name's Maddie Landon. I'm a private investigator looking into the disappearance of Katie Lewis."

"Did you say disappearance? What happened?" she said, sounding upset.

"That's what I'm trying to find out. I was just at the Vanderbilt Tennis facility and was told you were friendly with Katie. I was wondering if we could meet since I have some questions."

"We weren't that close."

"I understand, but it would be helpful if we could talk in person."

"I'm at work now. How about 5:30. There's a place on 74th and Broadway called Slate Café Upper West Side."

"Actually, I know the place. It's not too far from my office. I'll see you then."

CHAPTER 18

At 5:15 p.m., I locked up and headed out to meet Stacey Adam. Upon entering the Slate Café, I was greeted by long benches with leather backs lining both side walls. In the center of the floor were neatly arranged stools beneath a wooden countertop.

Stacey was already settled in against the left side wall when I arrived. I took a seat opposite her, a small square table positioned between us. I'm guessing Stacey was in her early thirties with dark, almost black straight hair that framed her oblong-shaped face. Her bright pink nails were perfectly manicured.

"Hi, Stacey. Glad to meet you," I said, shaking her hand. "My treat; what would you like?" I went up to the counter and ordered two cappuccinos and two blueberry muffins. The café had an extensive menu written on chalkboards, listing all kinds of breakfast items, sandwiches, and salads.

"We'll bring it to the table when it's ready," the nice young man taking my order said.

"I can't believe something has happened to Katie?" Stacey said when I sat down.

"We don't know at this point, but that's what I'm trying to find out. What can you tell me about her?"

The server came with our cappuccinos and muffins and left.

"Like I told you, I don't know her all that well, though a few times after our tennis lesson we went out for coffee.

I like Katie. The last time we saw each other, we were planning to get together for dinner."

"Do you remember when that was?"

"Maybe three weeks ago."

"When she hadn't been at the club in the last couple of weeks, did you wonder why?"

"Not really, since it's not that unusual to skip a week or two. I was going to call her if she hadn't shown up this week."

"Can you tell me what you discussed?"

"She had told me she'd been married and had left her husband."

"And did she say why?"

"She mentioned that he was extremely possessive, and it became too much for her living with someone so controlling. I suspect she might have been seeing someone else, but I'm not certain."

"What makes you say that?"

"She never came out and actually told me, but there were little hints here and there."

"Can you be more specific?"

"One day when we were having coffee, she mentioned she couldn't stay long. When I asked if she had a date, she simply smiled. I realized it wasn't my place to pry; if she wanted to share more, she would when she was ready."

"Your tennis instructor is quite handsome. Do you think she had her eye on him?"

"No, but I got the feeling he was quite enamored with her."

"What are you basing that on?"

"You could tell by the way he took his time when he was correcting her tennis. He tried not to show any favoritism, but it was apparent to me." Was Stacey jealous?

"How do you know she wasn't interested in him."

"She once told me that she felt uncomfortable when he got too close while giving her instructions on the court."

"Did she say anything to him?"

"As far as I know she didn't, and I doubt she would have made a scene in front of the other women."

"Is there anything else that you can recall?"

"One day after our clinic was over, I overheard him asking if she wanted a private lesson free of charge."

"Really! How could he manage that without anyone at the facility knowing about it?"

"I'm sure there are ways around it," she said in jest.

"Did you hear her response to Jake?"

"No, I'm sorry, I wish I had," she said, while picking at the crumbs on her plate.

"How long ago was this?"

"Maybe a couple of weeks ago."

"I was curious how someone on a teacher's salary can afford lessons here."

"Actually, the clinic lessons are only forty-five dollars. Are the police looking into her disappearance?"

"Not at the moment. There's not enough for them to warrant an investigation. Katie's parents hired me."

"Is there something I can do?"

"Here's my card. If you think of anything at all please call me. It could be a remark Katie said in passing that at the time didn't seem important. One other thing. Was there anyone else Jake had eyes on?"

"Let me think. There was one person, but she no longer takes lessons at the club."

"Would you happen to know why?"

"No. One day she just didn't show up."

"Do you know her name?"

"Her first name was Terri but I don't know her last name. Perhaps you can ask Leslie."

"I will. Thanks."

Could Terri have left because of Jake? I had to find out.

CHAPTER 19

My phone buzzed as I was walking home. "Hey, lover boy," I said when I saw it was Jesse calling. "Do you miss me yet?"

"If you were here, I would show you how much."

"Now you're talking my kind of language. Any luck finding your guy?"

"Not so far. Nobody's been very helpful. Either they don't know where he is or they're not talking. How's everything there?"

"I'm fine. The case is another story." I caught Jesse up to date. "I have no idea where she is or if she's still alive. I can't seem to get a grip on this."

"What about the husband. What's your take on him?"

"According to everyone I've spoken to he had a hard-on for her. He couldn't seem to let her go."

"But does that make him a killer?"

"Maybe not, but what if his mentality is, 'If I can't have her no one can.' That's a possibility, along with other scenarios."

"It sounds like the person she was taking tennis lessons from might have had some interest in her. Do you know anything about him? It could be a wild-goose chase, but as we know, we can't dismiss anything," Jesse said.

"I'm looking into him, but I also need to dig deeper into the husband. Perhaps a past girlfriend. He could have stalked other women."

"Be careful."

"Always."

"If only I could believe you."

"I love you. Hurry up and come back."

***

As soon as I walked through my apartment door, I made a beeline for the bottle of Cabernet Sauvignon waiting for me on my kitchen counter. With my glass in hand, I settled into my father's wingback chair, and my thoughts naturally drifted to him. My dad, a dedicated schoolteacher, would come home each day and sit in this chair, engrossed in *The New York Times*. We had a playful tradition where I would sneak up onto his lap and tickle his ear, and he would feign ignorance, playfully wondering aloud who could be tickling him. A smile spread across my face remembering those moments and the joy they brought me.

Two glasses of wine later, I was so tired I couldn't muster up the energy to put together something to eat. Instead, I had a bowl of cereal and went straight to bed.

***

When I woke up in the morning, my head was killing me. I swallowed two Tylenol and took a shower. Before walking into my office, I picked up an egg sandwich, home fries, and a large coffee. About an hour later I felt almost human. Scanning through the report I had originally pulled up on Paul Lewis, nothing jumped out at me. I picked up the phone and dialed Mr. Peterson's number.

"Mr. Peterson," I said when he answered. "It's Maddie Landon. I had a question. Does your son-in-law have any siblings?"

"Paul is an only child. Why?"

"What about a good friend?"

"Let me think a second. Yes, of course. He was his best man at their wedding, Charlie, Charlie something. Can I call you back when I get home? I believe I have it somewhere."

"Also, if you have a photo of him from their wedding, I would appreciate a copy. Just text it to me. Thanks."

Could Katie's husband have anything to do with Peter Crawford's murder? If he found out about the affair, would it make him angry enough to kill Crawford? But whoever did it, would they have left a witness alive?

CHAPTER 20

That evening I received a text from Mr. Peterson with Charlie's last name, contact number, and a photo. When I pulled up the report on Charlie Logan, it listed his age as thirty, married, and living in a condo on the east side in the twenties.

Looking at the photo, Charlie had light brown hair, a slightly hooked nose, and a dimple in his square chin. Definitely easy on the eyes. I decided to surprise Charlie since I didn't want him calling Paul Lewis prior to my visit. According to the report, Mr. Logan was a tax attorney working for a firm in midtown Manhattan. I thought it would be easier to drop in at his place of business rather than his home.

***

After my workout at the gym in the morning, I headed to Mr. Logan's office. When I walked into the building, I was told the firm was on the fifteenth floor. I located the staircase near the second set of elevators, and by the time I reached my destination, I was sucking air.

"Good morning," I said to the young man who was sitting behind the reception desk. He appeared to be a college student with a thick head of curly black hair and wire-rimmed glasses. If I was twenty years younger, I would have made a play for him.

"Hi, how can I help you?"

"I'd like to speak with Charlie Logan." I thought I would cut to the chase. "I don't have an appointment," I said, handing him my card.

"Very cool. People must tell you that all the time. I'm a student at John Jay Law Enforcement studying to become a forensic investigator. My name's Jeremy."

"Hi, Jeremy. Studying to be a forensic investigator must be very interesting."

"I'm hoping to work for the prosecutor's office one day."

"Well, give me a call when you get settled somewhere."

"I will," he said, perking up. "Mr. Logan," he said to the man walking out, "this woman is here to see you."

"Do we have an appointment that I don't know about?" he said, looking at me.

"No. It's about Katie Lewis. She's missing."

"Walk with me. I'm on my way to a meeting."

"Mr. Logan, Maddie Landon. I'm a private investigator," I said, as we stepped onto the elevator. I took a couple of deep breaths, hoping he wouldn't notice. Logan was solidly built. His clothes looked expensive, and I noticed the Rolex he had on his left hand. I wondered if it was real. "Would you mind giving me a few minutes before your meeting?"

He looked at his watch. "Why don't we grab a cup of coffee. I can give you fifteen."

We stopped at a Starbucks that was on the corner and grabbed a table. We dispensed with the coffee.

"So how do you know Paul?"

"We go way back. We met in high school. So what's going on?"

"The truth is I'm not sure. Katie's parents are worried since they haven't heard from their daughter in over a week and her phone is dead. I was told you're good friends with Paul."

"Yes, but what has this got to do with Katie?" Since I knew he was in a hurry, I didn't have much choice but to get right to the point.

"What can you tell me about their relationship?"

"I'm assuming you know they're separated. Paul loves Katie and I think he was trying to work things out with her."

"Did you know that Paul was stalking his wife?" Logan's eyes opened wide.

"Look, if you're going where I think you're going, let me stop you right there. Paul is crazy about Katie. He would never do anything to hurt her."

"But Katie isn't with Paul anymore, and from what I've been told, she doesn't want anything to do with him. I've heard from several people that he was very possessive of her during their marriage."

"Where are you getting this from? Her friend Gail? I wouldn't trust anything she said. She never liked Paul. Did you know she was against the marriage from the beginning? Did Paul tell you that Katie was going out at night, never telling him where she went? Who knows what the hell she was doing. Maybe you should focus your investigation somewhere else instead of on Paul."

I didn't want to get into a pissing match with Logan. I was here to get information. "Look, I'm sorry if I came on too strong. I'm trying to figure out what happened to Katie. Can you think of anything?"

"Okay. About a month ago, Katie called me. She was concerned because Paul was having trouble dealing with the separation and she asked me if I would talk to him."

"And did you?"

"Yes. He told me he loved her and was just trying to get her to hear what he had to say. I told him to back off but I guess he didn't listen."

"I know you're good friends with Paul and you're loyal to him, but do you think he could have had anything to do with her disappearance?"

"Paul may be overzealous when it comes to Katie, but he would never harm her. I'm sorry, but I have to leave for my appointment."

"Thank you for your time. Here's my card. If you remember anything at all please call me."

I watched him as he was leaving, knowing I would probably never hear from him again. What did I expect? He wouldn't betray his best friend even if he had doubts about Paul.

CHAPTER 21

Heading back, I realized Noah's birthday party was on Sunday and I still hadn't gotten him a birthday present. I stopped to check my phone where the nearest toy store was located. Do they even exist anymore? Apparently they do, since I found one not far from my office.

The toy store was buzzing with the chatter of kids walking alongside their parents, pleading for this toy or that one. I went in search of a salesperson since I had no clue what a three-year-old would want. I caught the attention of a young girl who looked barely out of her teens. She was very bubbly and seemed eager to help.

"I'm looking for a birthday present for a three-year-old boy. Do you have any suggestions?"

"I do." She brought me over to the bike area, and showed me a small bike that had no pedals.

"That's interesting. How does it work?"

"The children use their feet, which teaches them balance and steering skills. Kids love them."

Though I asked the price, I knew I was going to get it for Noah no matter what the cost. I'm not sure his parents would approve of him riding in the house, but I knew Noah would love it. I had the store ship the bike to my apartment.

***

With my feet up on my office desk, I was mulling over my next step. Could Charlie Logan be right? Did Gail Davis,

Katie's best friend, have it in for Paul? I was pretty sure Gail wasn't making it up. Besides, there were too many calls from Paul to Katie listed on her phone records. I would bet that somewhere in his past there was another woman he also stalked. All I had to do was find her. I saw an email from my source telling me the phone number I gave him was a dead end. Most likely a burner phone. Though I thought that might be the case, it still bummed me out.

I was curious if the Yonkers Police Department had any leads on who killed Peter Crawford. The tricky part was how to get information from them without bringing up Katie's name. I was fairly certain that Marty from the motel mentioned a woman Crawford was with that night. However, since she stayed in the car when he registered, I was counting on the fact that Marty wouldn't be able to provide a description of her, even after I showed him a photo of her. By this time the police would have pulled Crawford's cell phone records and her number would have popped up.

The desk sergeant who answered at the station gave me the name of the detective in charge of the case, but told me Detective Stone wasn't in and to call back in an hour.

In looking through Paul Lewis's database report, there was a prior address from a few years back before he was married to Katie. I scribbled it down and gave Detective Stone a call as I was on my way out.

"How can I help you?" Detective Stone said when I was finally put through to him.

"My name's Maddie Landon. I'm a private investigator and former detective with the NYPD. I heard that someone by the name of Peter Crawford was found dead at the Horizon Motel."

"And what is your interest in the case?"

"I was going to ask him a few questions regarding an investigation I'm working on, but of course that's impossible now. I was just wondering if you had any leads."

"As you know, motel rooms are difficult to get any prints from. We know he was struck by a blow to the back of the head. We're pretty sure the weapon was a lamp that was in the room, but our forensic team is still working on it."

"Could you tell if there was a struggle?"

"I really can't talk about the case any further."

"I understand. Can you at least tell me if you have any suspects."

"How does your investigation involve Peter Crawford?"

Damn. "I'm working on a missing person case and my subject may have known Mr. Crawford."

"What is this person's name?"

"Katie Lewis."

"And how did they know each other?"

I didn't feel the need to be completely truthful with Detective Stone. "I'm not sure at this point, that's why I wanted to talk to Mr. Crawford. Well, I appreciate your time," I said, and I hung up.

Even if he already knew it was Katie, he would have kept that information to himself. How long would it take before Detective Stone found out about her involvement with Peter Crawford?

CHAPTER 22

At 4:00 p.m. I headed up to the Bronx where Paul Lewis had lived before marrying Katie. It was a six-story brick building with air conditioners sticking out of the windows. The street was narrow with apartment buildings on both sides and trees that appeared scrawny, thin, and bare. I squeezed my Honda Civic in between two big SUVs and entered the vestibule. I tried the door to the lobby but it was locked. Checking the directory, I rang the superintendent's buzzer.

"Hello, who's there?" I heard through some static.

"Can you let me in? I need to talk with the super." The buzzer sounded and I walked into the lobby. According to the directory, the super lived in a basement apartment. I found the stairs and walked down one flight, turning right and finding the laundry room down the hall.

"Excuse me," I said to the woman unloading her clothes from the washing machine. "Can you tell me where the superintendent lives?"

"He's just down the hall. Make a left out of here and you'll run right into his apartment."

"Thank you." Though my building has a laundry room, I'm so lazy I drop my clothes off at the laundromat a few blocks from my apartment. Let them have the pleasure of washing my clothes.

I made a left and found the super's apartment at the end of the hallway. I rang the bell and a short, stocky woman, probably in her fifties, wearing an apron over what looked like a flowered housedress, opened the door.

"How can I help you? The super isn't here right now, but I'm his wife," she said in a friendly manner.

"Something smells wonderful." It did, but nothing like a little flattery to help the situation.

"I'm baking an apple pie."

"I'm envious. I'm a terrible baker."

"I'm sure if you put your mind to it you can learn. Now, how can I help you?" she said again.

I gave her my card. "I'm trying to get in contact with a man by the name of Paul Lewis. It's regarding an automobile accident that happened a few years back and I need to talk to him." A little white lie comes with the territory.

"Mr. Lewis hasn't lived here for a few years."

"Oh! Do you know where he lives now?"

"Maybe Diana might know."

"Who's Diana?"

"That was his girlfriend. She still lives in the building." I could feel my pulse beating a little faster. A stroke of good luck.

"Do you know why he left?" I said very nonchalantly.

"You'd have to ask her. She lives in 4G."

"Thank you for your time."

It was nearing 5:00 p.m. There was no answer when I rang Diana's doorbell and knocked for good measure. I decided not to leave my card. As I was walking toward the stairs, a young woman was getting off the elevator.

"Excuse me. Is your name Diana by any chance?"

"Who's asking?"

"My name's Maddie Landon. I'm a private investigator," I said, handing her my card. She looked at it for a moment. "Do you think we could talk?"

"I don't know you. What is this about?"

I settled for the truth. "I'm investigating the disappearance of a woman who was married to Paul Lewis." Her jaw dropped slightly.

"I think we better go inside."

Paul had excellent taste in women. He definitely had a type; very dark brown hair, large eyes, slender with porcelain white skin. Diana's apartment was small, but neat, with a galley kitchen done all in white. There were hardwood floors throughout. The living room was decorated in shabby chic style with a white couch with decorative pastel-colored flowered pillows on each side. On one end of the couch was an antique end table and on the other side was a huge palm tree. The mint green console table behind the couch had distressed markings, giving it the appearance of being old.

"Can I get you something to drink? I'm going to have a glass of wine."

"Sure. I'll join you," I said, as I settled in on the couch.

When Diana sat down opposite me on a light blue upholstered chair, she said, "Are you looking into Paul as a suspect?"

"As of this moment, I've had no indication that anything has happened to her. I'm just investigating all possibilities. Paul and his wife are separated. I did learn from a friend of Paul's wife that he had been harassing her after the breakup. He wouldn't stop calling her and was showing up at her apartment unannounced at all different times. When I spoke with Mr. Lewis, he told me he was hoping to reconcile with his wife."

"Sounds vaguely familiar."

"What do you mean?"

"I'd have to start from the beginning."

CHAPTER 23

"I was young when I first met Paul. He was eighteen and I was seventeen. We knew each other from the neighborhood and started dating. I was going into my senior year of high school and Paul was in his freshman year at Bernard Baruch, a city college in downtown Manhattan, where he was majoring in business.

"Everything was really good between us, and I thought I was in love with Paul. As I said I was young when we first started going out. Though I dated somewhat before Paul, he was my first serious boyfriend. When he graduated, we moved in together. I was working part time as a secretary while going to Bronx Community College. At first everything was great, but then Paul's behavior changed. If I didn't come home right after my last class, he would interrogate me when I got back."

"Like how?"

"'Where were you? Your class ended two hours ago! Were you with anyone? Who were you with?' Maybe it was a little flattering at first that he was jealous, but it got to the point where every time I walked in the door, I had to brace myself for what was to come. Besides the interrogation, it was his tone; it was a little scary. I told him nothing was going on and that he would have to trust me, but that didn't seem to make a difference. I finally said I couldn't live like this, always under suspicion, and that if he didn't change, one of us would have to move out."

"How did that go over?"

"He begged for my forgiveness and said it wouldn't happen again, but of course it did. It took a while, but I finally got him to move out, and I thought that was the end of it. The first couple of weeks I hadn't heard from him, but then the calls started. At first, there were only one or two each day, mostly in the evening, but then they increased to all hours. I didn't know what to do."

"What were the calls like?"

"Sometimes he would tell me how much he loved me and missed me. Other times he would call me names and tell me what a horrible person I was. I eventually told my father what was going on and he must have threatened Paul since I never heard from him again."

"Was Paul ever violent?"

"Not really. Once, he raised his hand as if he was going to hit me, but instead, punched the wall."

"Is there anyone else that he was close to that maybe I could speak with?"

"It's not as if Paul had a lot of friends. I only knew his friend Charlie Logan."

"I already spoke to him. He wasn't very helpful. Either he had no idea what his friend was like or he didn't want to betray him."

"Most likely the latter. Paul and Charlie go back a long way."

"Well, if you think of anything else, please call me."

"I will and I hope his wife is alright."

***

As I was starting my car, I saw Jesse was calling.

"Hey. I just bought Noah a bicycle with no pedals for his birthday. Apparently it's the rage."

"I wish I could be there. Can you make it from both of us and I'll give you half?"

"I guess I can trust you for the money," I said jokingly.

"Listen, something's come up. I really hate to spring this on you."

"What's going on?" I said, as I got this queasy feeling in the pit of my stomach.

"Karen just called me. According to the doctors, her mother is dying and most likely she won't make it through the end of the week. She needs to go down to Florida to be with her mother at the hospital and she has no one to leave Leo with. I can't come back yet. Is there any way he can stay with you for a few days?"

"What am I going to do with him during the day?" I was starting to sweat. "I can't take him with me while I'm working. Does Karen even know you were going to ask me? I don't get the feeling I'm a fan of hers."

"Don't be ridiculous. She doesn't really know you."

"That's comforting. Where would he sleep?"

"He has a sleeping bag, but he can always sleep on the couch. Don't worry, kids are very resilient. I know this is a really big ask but I don't know what else to do."

"You are going to owe me really big, and I can't guarantee this kid is going to be alive when you get back." *Maybe it's me who won't get out of this alive.*

"I have faith in you," Jesse said. I can picture him smiling.

"When do I have to get him?"

"Now. Karen is taking a flight out tonight. Leo will be with the next-door neighbor."

"Are you kidding me. It's after 6:00 p.m. Can't he stay with the neighbor tonight and I'll pick him up in the morning?"

"Let me see what I can work out. Sit tight."

When we hung up, I tried to calm myself. I was right in the thick of my investigation and I didn't need any distractions, especially one that involved taking care of a kid. I turned off the engine and quickly dialed Annie, hoping she wasn't with a client.

"Thank God," I said when she answered.

"What's the matter? Are you alright?"

I went on to tell Annie my conversation with Jesse.

"This would be really funny if it was anyone but you."

"What am I going to do?"

"Okay, don't panic. Let's think this through. What about Noah's babysitter. She takes care of him during the day while Sophie is working. If you paid her, I bet she would take care of Leo as well. You would just have to okay it with Sophie first."

"You're a genius."

"I've never been called that before, but I'll take it."

I called Sophie as soon as I hung up. I explained the situation and she said it was fine with her and that Marla would love the extra money. I breathed a sigh of relief.

CHAPTER 24

While waiting for Jesse to call me, I reflected on the decision I made last year to search for my birth parents. It wasn't an easy choice. From a young age, my adoptive parents had told me about my adoption, and I often imagined the worst—that my birth parents were likely junkies who had discarded me like garbage. So when I finally uncovered the truth, it was a great relief. Unfortunately, it also brought pain; my birth mother had passed away a few years earlier, and my birth father never knew I existed. My birth mother's sister, Lucy, explained that their parents were strict Catholics and extremely religious. When they discovered their sixteen-year-old daughter, Lydia, was pregnant, they sent her to live with an aunt in another state. After I was born, they forced her to give me up for adoption. Although my mother eventually married, she never had any other children and never fully recovered from the heartache of giving her baby away. My birth father lives in California, and while we don't see each other often, we talk on the phone regularly.

"Hey," I said when I saw it was Jesse calling me back.

"You can pick him up in the morning as long as you're there by 9:00 a.m. A car service is coming at 9:30 a.m. to take Mrs. Weinstein to the airport."

"Tell her I'll be there by 9:00. Oh, and by the way, Noah's babysitter is going to watch Leo during the day."

"I love you."

"Yeah! Yeah! Yeah! Me too."

***

In the morning, I took a quick shower and stopped to get coffee on my way up to Chester, Connecticut. I wasn't thrilled about this arrangement since I'd never had to take care of anyone except myself, and especially not a five-year-old kid.

For a small town, Chester has several upscale boutiques and restaurants. The garden apartment complex where Leo lived was very clean and beautifully kept, with colorful flowers planted in front. The buildings were three stories high and each apartment had its own terrace. I knocked on Mrs. Weinstein's door. The woman standing in front of me was tall and stout, maybe in her late sixties. Her blondish-gray hair looked as if it had just been styled at the salon. Her tortoiseshell glasses were sitting low on her nose.

"Come in. You must be Maddie. Leo has talked about you. He is such a darling and I wish I could look after him, but I'm leaving soon to visit my daughter in Virginia for a few days. Can I get you anything before you head back? Leo has already had breakfast."

"No, thank you. I'll eat something when we get home."

"Leo, Maddie's here. All his stuff is in his backpack, except for his sleeping bag."

"Hi, Maddie. My daddy says I'm going to be spending a few days with you. I get to miss school. Isn't that so cool?"

"Yeah, really cool," I said, trying to keep a positive outlook. "Thank you for keeping him overnight."

"Bye, Mrs. Weinstein."

"Have fun with Maddie."

Leo looked a lot like Jesse. He had Jesse's dark brown hair, large dark eyes with long eyelashes I envied.

"Are you allowed to sit in the front," I said to Leo since, honestly, I had no idea where a five-year-old should sit.

"Yes, as long as I'm buckled in."

"Okay!"

"Are we going to your office?"

"No, but I have something better planned. A nice woman by the name of Marla is going to look after you during the day. She'll take you to the park and do lots of other fun stuff with you. Also, my cousin Noah will be with you part of the time."

"How old is he?"

"He's going to be three on Sunday."

"He's a baby. I don't want to play with a baby. I'm going to be six very soon. Why can't I come with you?" Was this a temper tantrum?

"Because I'm going to be interviewing people and they might feel uncomfortable if you're with me." Leo didn't say anything. Maybe he was thinking of ways to kill me in my sleep.

"Did you know I live in a big apartment building in New York City. Have you ever been to New York?"

"One time. My mother took me to this gigantic Lego store. Then we went to see the Christmas tree where there were people ice skating. It looked like fun."

"I thought you might be interested in seeing more of the city on Saturday unless you had something else in mind. Maybe even take a ride on the subway."

"Really!" I glanced over and saw the excitement on his face. If that was all it took to make him happy, I'd ride the subway all day long, even if it meant having to be stuck in a subway car at the mercy of the subway system.

When we got to Sophie's brownstone on the east side in the sixties, I parked my car. As we were walking, I watched as Leo looked all around. At one point, he tugged at my hand. "Look at that man, his hair is purple and green," Leo said, giggling. The city was certainly going to be an intriguing place for him.

When Jesse and I first met, he told me marriage and children had eluded him, so when he found out about Leo just a few months ago, it was a shock to Jesse. It wasn't something either of us bargained for. As it turns out, when I was in my early twenties, I had developed endometriosis, and it left me unable to have children. I had come to terms with it, but I wasn't sure how Jesse would feel. When I finally got up the nerve to tell him, he said it didn't matter to him. Being around Leo the past few months has definitely been an experience. Though I'm still not completely comfortable around him, he seems to be okay with me.

Dropping Leo off with Marla was no minor matter. I had to promise I'd be back by 6:00 p.m. and take him to McDonald's for dinner. Though Marla was very warm and welcoming, she was still a stranger to him. The expression on his face when I walked away made me feel like a monster.

CHAPTER 25

I realized as I was driving to my office that I was in desperate need of speaking to my therapist, Dr. Goldberg, who I had been seeing for over a year. I called her office and her receptionist said she could see me at 4:00 p.m. today.

It was Annie who first kept badgering me about seeing a therapist. Before Jesse, I had several boyfriends who were short-lived. With Jesse, it was the first time I could see myself in a serious relationship and it scared me. When my adoptive parents died, I knew that at any moment you could lose your whole world. I never wanted to feel that pain again so I built an imaginary wall that kept me safe. I knew if I kept that wall I could lose him.

My first call when I got into my office was to Leslie at the Vanderbilt Tennis Club. I was eager to connect with Terri. According to Stacey Adam, Terri suddenly stopped coming to her tennis lessons. Stacey thought Jake may have taken an interest in Terri, and I wanted to know if the two situations were connected.

"Front desk, Leslie speaking."

"Leslie, it's Maddie Landon. We met a few days ago."

"Of course. Any news on Katie?"

"No, not yet, but that's not why I'm calling. I was told a woman by the name of Terri just stopped coming to your club. Would you happen to know why?"

"People stop coming for all different reasons. They usually don't tell us and we don't ask."

"I would really like to find out why. Do you think you could tell me her last name?"

"But what connection could there possibly be?"

I had to be really careful about what I said to Leslie since I didn't want Jake's name coming up in our conversation.

"I don't know, but if it's remotely related to Katie's disappearance, that's something I need to find out." I wasn't sure if she accepted my explanation, but I wanted to know Terri's last name. If this worried Leslie, perhaps she would share it with me. Leslie put me on hold. I was still holding five minutes later. Was someone telling her they couldn't give out that information?

"Maddie, sorry I took so long." *Please tell me you have her last name.* "It took me a while to find her name since she was no longer in our active files on our computer."

"That's okay."

"Terri's last name is Hartley. I have an email address I can give you, but I really don't feel comfortable giving out her home address and telephone number."

"I understand and I appreciate your cooperation."

"Please let me know she's alright."

"I will." I felt slightly guilty that I wasn't completely honest with her, but not enough to lose sleep over.

I thought I would email Terri Hartley first and see if she replied. If not, I would have to track her down. In my email, I gave her just enough information to prompt her to respond. After several modifications, I finally pressed the send button. Now I just had to wait.

I was wondering how Leo was doing and was debating whether to call Marla when I heard a ding. I saw it was an email from Terri. "Can we meet at 2:00 p.m. at the Starbucks on Third Avenue and 63rd Street?" I answered back in the affirmative.

From Terri's description, I recognized her as soon as she walked into Starbucks. She was petite with an athletic body. Her straight red hair was cut short with bangs. When she got closer, I noticed her large hazel-colored eyes and a slightly turned-up nose with a few scattered freckles.

"Thank you for meeting me, Terri. Can I get you anything to drink?"

We both ordered cappuccinos, and since I was starving, I threw in a ham and Swiss on a baguette. I retrieved our order and joined Terri at the table.

"You were kind of vague in your email. What is this about?"

I gave her my card. "I'm investigating a case involving a missing woman who was taking tennis lessons at the Vanderbilt Tennis Club."

"Can you tell me her name?"

"It's Katie Lewis." The look on her face told me she knew Katie.

"We were both in Jake's tennis clinic, though I left a few weeks after Kate joined us."

"Why did you leave?"

"Before I answer, what has my leaving have to do with Katie?"

"I'm not sure if it does, but I was told that Jake seemed to have an interest in her and possibly you." I waited for her response.

"You think Jake had something to do with her disappearance?"

"I don't know at this point, but I have to look into all avenues. I was hoping you might be able to fill me in on your interactions with him."

Terri was quiet. I could see on her face she was debating what to tell me.

"After our group lessons, Jake always made it a point to chat with me, even offering to give me private lessons at no cost. Initially, I felt flattered by his attention; Jake can be quite charming. However, I was careful not to encourage him since I had a boyfriend."

"Did you tell him that?"

"Yes, but it didn't seem to dissuade him."

"Did you mention it to anyone who works at the club?"

"I should have but I didn't want him to get into trouble, and I thought I could handle the situation myself. It finally got to the point where it wasn't fun being there anymore, so I left and went someplace else."

"Did he try and contact you after you were no longer there?"

"He called me a few times trying to get me to come back."

"Did he ever ask you out?" I noticed Terri fidgeting, playing with the spoon on the table. What was she hiding?

"This doesn't go any further, right?"

"Absolutely. I promise you."

"It was stupid of me and I don't know why I did it, but I went out with him once. He kept asking and I finally relented."

"Can you tell me what happened?"

"At first, Jake was a complete gentleman. He took me to a quaint Italian restaurant, where we talked about various topics—my interests, his future plans, and other lighthearted topics. However, as we were leaving, he asked if I wanted to come back to his place. I told him no and explained that I couldn't see him again. His demeanor completely changed; he became angry and even called me a tease. That's when I left him standing by the restaurant and grabbed a cab back to my apartment."

"How come you decided not to go out with him again?"

"As I mentioned, I have a boyfriend and I felt guilty for cheating on him. Also, I got this bad vibe from Jake."

"What kind of bad vibe?"

"Not quite sure. Were you ever out with someone and you thought they were trying a little too hard to impress you? It felt forced. I can't explain it any other way; it just didn't feel right. As it turned out something really weird happened when I got home. When I went to close the drapes in my apartment, I saw him standing outside."

"That is very strange. Did he see you?"

"He did, but when I looked a few minutes later, he was gone. It was really creepy."

"Did he try to contact you after your date?"

"He called and texted several times but I blocked him. After a while, I never heard from him again."

"Thank you for telling me the truth."

Did Jake focus his attention on Katie because Terri had left? Maybe I was grasping at straws, but I was getting a bad feeling about this guy. Right now I couldn't dwell on it since I needed to get to my therapy session with Dr. Goldberg.

CHAPTER 26

Dr. Goldberg's office was on the first floor in an apartment building in the mid-sixties on the West Side. I sat in her waiting room, my right leg shaking. When I first began therapy, I had no idea what to expect. It took me several weeks before I felt comfortable enough to open up about the issues that had been haunting me since childhood.

Though it was hard for me in the beginning, Dr. Goldberg had this way about her that made me feel safe. Matronly looking, she was like the grandmother everyone wished they had.

"Come in, Maddie," Dr. Goldberg said.

I sat in my usual spot, a wooden-frame chair with a blue-cushioned seat and Dr. Goldberg sat across from me in a gray club chair.

"What's going on, Maddie?"

"I'm not sure where to begin. Jesse and I were looking at apartments with a realtor a few days ago and I started panicking. I felt trapped, and was having a hard time breathing."

"Like how you felt when you were trapped in the backseat of your parents' car the night they died."

What she said hit me hard; I couldn't hold back the tears.

"Why are you crying, Maddie?"

"I still have dreams about that night. I wake up, my whole body shaking."

"Can you say more about the dreams?"

"I don't remember much; I do remember yelling out to my parents, but there was no answer. I began to panic."

"Do you recall anything else?"

"I think there were these big men dressed in black talking to me through a window. I was crying and then everything goes blank."

"I believe those men were firemen who came to rescue you. Maddie, you're not that twelve-year-old girl anymore. You're not trapped. If your worst fear came true, and somehow Jesse was no longer in your life, it wouldn't devastate you because you're not alone. You have people in your life who care about you. You're stronger than you think."

Her words stuck in my throat.

"Did you mention your doubts to Jesse?"

"No. I couldn't. I was afraid. I told Annie. She said it's okay if I wasn't ready to move in with him, but I had to be willing to accept the consequences if Jesse walked away."

"How did you feel about what she said?"

"I don't want to lose him." The moment the words came out of my mouth, I realized what I had to do, even if it meant letting him go.

CHAPTER 27

As I headed to pick up Leo, I felt a sense of relief. I understood that the conversation with Jesse would be difficult, but if we were to have a chance at all, it was a conversation we had to face.

As promised, Leo and I picked up hamburgers and fries at McDonald's. On the car ride back to my place, Leo was quiet. I should have tried engaging him in conversation, but between the case and my session with Dr. Goldberg, my mind wasn't functioning in full gear.

I parked the car in my garage and helped Leo up with his stuff. I was feeling a little anxious. Was I afraid I would screw things up so badly with a five-year-old that he'd tell his mother and Jesse that he hated me?

"So what did you do with Marla and Noah today?" I said, as we were eating.

"We went to Central Park. Did you know they have a zoo with sea lions and monkeys? Marla said when the weather is warmer, we can ride in one of the rowboats."

"That sounds like fun."

"Marla bought me a hot dog from a man who was in a steel box selling them on the street. It was yummy."

Oh great. A hot dog for lunch and a hamburger and french fries for dinner. Is this considered child abuse? "How about some salad?"

"Do I have to? My mother doesn't make me. It's yucky."

I didn't want to force him. I wasn't going to win any brownie points if I did.

"Are you going to marry my father?" he said, as he was busy dipping a french fry into a mound of ketchup.

The question threw me. I wasn't sure what to say as I took a gulp of my wine. "I don't know, Leo."

"Don't you love him?"

"Just because two people love each other doesn't mean they have to marry. Each couple does it the way they think is best for them. How is your hamburger?" I said, attempting to distract Leo, hoping he wouldn't ask any more questions I might not be up to answering.

"What time do I have to go to bed?"

"What time do you go to bed at home?"

"When I don't have school, my mother lets me stay up as long as I want to."

I doubted Leo was telling me the truth, but I didn't want to challenge him. "Well, I guess you can stay up until I'm ready to go to bed." I could tell he liked that answer since I saw a little smile cross his face.

"I know how to play gin rummy. Do you want to play?" he said enthusiastically.

I was tired, but I didn't have the heart to say no. "Why don't you get into your pajamas and brush your teeth while I clean up. I think I have a deck of cards somewhere around here."

After five games of gin rummy, Leo winning two, I could see he was having a hard time keeping his eyes open. It was 10:00 p.m. I laid him down on the couch and covered him. I was so tired I quickly changed and plopped into bed.

Something was touching my arm. My instincts kicked in and I jumped. I saw Leo's big dark brown eyes staring at me. "What's the matter?" I said almost in a panic.

"Can I sleep in your room? I don't want to sleep in the living room all by myself." I let out a sigh of relief.

"Why don't you get your sleeping bag and put it on the floor by my bed." After he was settled in, I closed my eyes and was fast asleep.

***

I almost stepped on Leo as I got out of bed in the morning. While he was still asleep, I showered and put on the coffee maker before waking him up.

"How about some Cheerios and milk?" I said. The truth is, I had no other breakfast food unless you considered a stale donut a breakfast item.

"I love Cheerios." Score one for the team.

"Why don't you shower first. I left a towel by the sink, and if you need any help, let me know."

"I'm not a baby. I shower by myself at home."

My phone was ringing. "Hello."

"Am I speaking with Maddie Landon?"

"Who is this?"

"This is Detective Rubin Stone. I need to see you in my office by 11:00 a.m. today."

CHAPTER 28

After dropping Leo off at Sophie's, I headed up to Yonkers. I knew that Marty from the motel would have been more than happy to tell them of my interest in the dead man, especially after the way I treated him. Maybe Paul Crawford's wife mentioned I had been asking about her husband. I had to think of a plausible story since I knew he would bring up Katie Lewis's name again.

When I arrived at the Yonkers Police Station, I announced my presence to the desk sergeant. Ten minutes later, I was sitting in front of Detective Rubin Stone. Detective Stone was at least 6 feet 3 inches tall, medium build, with thick, wavy red hair, and a bulbous nose. His professional demeanor meant he was all business.

"When we last spoke, I don't believe you were very forthcoming. I would like you to tell me again what your interest in the case is, Ms. Landon."

"As I told you, it involves a woman by the name of Katie Lewis who is missing. I was informed that she may have known the person who was killed at the motel. Otherwise, I have no information on this person or what happened to him."

"When I spoke to the clerk at the motel, he told me you were very interested in Peter Crawford. It seems like you went to an awful lot of trouble for someone who your missing person barely knew."

"I'm not sure what her involvement was with Peter Crawford. All I know at this point is that someone mentioned she met him at a bar. I was just trying to find out from the clerk on duty if he had seen my subject. Look, I want to be cooperative, but I really don't know anything else. If I did, I would tell you." I'm pretty sure he didn't buy my story, but what choice did he have.

"Well, if that's all, I'll be going."

"Don't go too far. I may need to ask you some follow-up questions. If I find out you've been withholding information pertinent to my case, there will be hell to pay." If looks could kill, I'd be dead.

"You know where to find me. By the way, did you make any headway on Mr. Crawford's death?"

"Have a nice day, Ms. Landon."

So much for police camaraderie. What did I expect. I had the feeling he knew I wasn't telling him everything. As I was heading to my office, my phone buzzed.

"Ms. Landon, it's Katie's mother. I have to show you something. It's important."

***

Instead of going back to the city, I traveled north to Dorothy Peterson's house in Crestwood, only ten minutes from where I was in Yonkers. Dorothy Peterson opened the door before I even had a chance to knock.

"Come in," she said, sounding excited. She brought me into the kitchen. Though it looked as if it hadn't been renovated in quite a few years, it was immaculate. The green-tiled floor matched the color of the stove and the refrigerator.

"Look." She showed me her phone and the text message she received. "This means that Katie is alive," Mrs. Peterson said, her eyes watering.

The message read: *Mom, sorry if I haven't returned your calls. I still need some more time. I'm fine, so don't worry about me. Love, Katie.*

Though Mrs. Peterson believed the message came from her daughter, I had this terrible feeling that it wasn't sent by Katie. If I was right, then Katie was either dead or in serious trouble.

"Is there anything in the message that seems odd to you?" I said.

"What do you mean?" she said, annoyed at my question.

"Well, for instance, is this how Katie would write a text? Does this sound like her?"

"What are you implying?"

"Just take another quick look and see if there's anything unusual or strange about the text message."

"No, as far as I can tell, Katie wrote it." I knew she wanted to believe it came from Katie.

"To be honest, we can't assume Katie wrote this." Mrs. Peterson's face dropped.

"Who else would it come from?" And then it registered. "OH MY GOD! NO! Please tell me it can't be."

"At this point we don't have any definitive information about Katie. Let's not jump to any conclusions or make any assumptions until we know more."

Mrs. Peterson's face went pale. I had dashed her hopes that her daughter may be alive.

"I know it's not easy, but you have to remain positive. I'm still not convinced that anything has happened to Katie."

"Are there any leads? What about Paul? You said he was stalking her."

"He was, and it turns out he exhibited the same behavior with his last girlfriend. So much so that she broke up with him."

"If he's that crazy, maybe he did something to Katie."

"I'm still investigating. I'll keep you updated when I have more news."

"My husband and I thought you would have found Katie by now. You have to try harder. Please! We're worried sick and my husband is not well. He has a heart condition and I'm afraid something might happen to him."

"Believe me when I say I'm doing everything I can to find Katie. Unfortunately, you can't always rush these things. Just be a little more patient. I know it's difficult."

I was glad to get out of there. Though the air was chilly, I was sweating and my heart was racing. I got into my car, sat quietly while taking deep breaths, trying to calm myself. I couldn't let the pressure get to me. The only thing I could do now was to keep investigating and hope something would break soon.

CHAPTER 29

My phone buzzed as I was turning onto the Bronx River Parkway, heading back to my office.

"Hey, babe. Is my son still alive?"

"Very funny. Though with my parenting skills, anything's possible. I have no idea what I'm doing."

"You're too hard on yourself. You can't screw him up that easily."

"Good to know. Don't take this the wrong way, but when are you coming home?"

"You miss me?"

"Yeah! That's it. Now answer the question," I said, grinning.

"I have a lead I'm running down now. With any luck, I should know more in a day or two."

"I want you to know I took the elevator instead of the stairs just so I wouldn't traumatize Leo with my own phobia."

"I'm proud of you. How's it going otherwise?"

"Well, he told me he was allowed to stay up as late as he wanted when there was no school. I didn't argue the point."

"There is one principle all kids live by, especially boys."

"And what is that?"

"Whatever they can get away with, they will. Only pick the battles worth fighting for. Otherwise, let it go."

"How do you know so much about kids?"

"For one, I was a kid myself and two, I still remember what it was like."

"Have you spoken to Karen?"

"Yes. They don't expect her mother to live more than another day or two. She's already hired a realtor and someone to sell the furniture in her mother's apartment, except for what she's going to take. The body will be shipped to the funeral home up here, and Karen will be back in another few days. Listen, I should be back by Monday. I'll come right to you and take Leo back with me."

"Don't worry. I'll manage."

"I know this was a lot to dump on you, especially since you've never been alone with Leo. I'll show you my appreciation when I get back."

"Looking forward to it. Love you."

"Right back at you. Gotta go."

I was sitting in my office, contemplating my next move. I hadn't spoken to any neighbors in Katie's apartment building yet, and I was hoping someone heard or saw something that could help with my investigation.

I picked up my phone and dialed Sophie's number.

"Hey, Maddie," she said. "How did everything go last night with Leo?"

"I'm muddling through. It's hard to deny him anything."

"When it's not your kid it's like walking on hot coals. Don't worry about it."

"I hate to ask but I need a big favor. I have to canvass neighbors on my case, and the best time to do it is in the evening. Is there any chance Leo can stay a few extra hours?"

"No problem. He can have dinner with us, and if you want, he can sleep over. Noah would love having Leo's company."

As tempting as that sounded, I didn't want to impose. "Maybe I should take him back with me. He doesn't have his pajamas or a change of clothes for tomorrow."

"I have an extra toothbrush, and one day wearing the same clothes won't kill him. He'll be fine."

"Thanks, Sophie. By the way, what time is Noah's party on Sunday?"

"Two o'clock, but come whenever."

***

At 6:30 p.m. I headed downtown to Katie's apartment building. I squeezed into a spot about a block away and waited outside the front door for someone to come out. A minute later I spotted an elderly gentleman leaving and slithered in before the door closed.

I climbed the steps to the fourth floor and knocked on the door that was to the right of Katie's apartment. The peephole opened. "Who is it?"

"My name's Maddie Landon, and I'm looking into the disappearance of your neighbor, Katie Lewis."

"Do you have some identification?" The door creaked open, still secured by the chain.

I reached into my pocket and pulled out my private investigator's laminated license, presenting it to her. After a moment's hesitation, she closed the door briefly, removed the chain, and then opened the door fully.

"I'm sorry to bother you. I'm canvassing the building, and I was wondering if I can ask you a few questions?"

"Please come in. I've been so worried about her."

CHAPTER 30

"I'm Sandra Tompkins." Sandra was tall with an angular face and a model's figure. Her brown curls came down past her shoulders. "Let's sit in the living room."

Where Katie's place looked like it had been thrown together with odd pieces, Sandra's apartment could have been featured in *House & Garden*. The furniture didn't look expensive, but she certainly had an eye for decorating. All the furniture was white, including a leather sofa. What I really loved were all the accent pieces that were full of vibrant colors. The white walls were adorned with large black and white photos that were taken of ordinary people in different outdoor settings.

"Did you take these photos? They're great," I said.

"Yes. I love to go out and take snapshots of ordinary people in everyday settings that I think are interesting. It takes me away from the stress of my everyday life. Would you like something to drink? I'm going to have a glass of white wine. Can I interest you?" Sandra said.

"Two things I never say no to, coffee and wine. Your apartment is lovely. Are you an interior decorator?"

"Thank you, but no. I'm finishing up my masters in psychology, and I work part-time at a boutique a few blocks from here."

"You mentioned you were worried about Katie. Are you friends with her?"

"We're always there for each other, even with our busy schedules. Between work and school, I hardly have time to socialize, but we make it a point to share what's happening in our lives. If she has a problem, she knows she can come to me, and I do the same. Because I'm home at night burning the midnight oil studying, Katie knows I'm up late if she needs to talk."

"Why do you think she confides in you?"

"Katie knows she could tell me anything and I won't judge her," she said, as she handed me a glass of wine.

"Do you think she went away for a few days like she told her parents and the school?"

"Absolutely not. She would have told me," she said indignantly.

I wasn't as sure as Sandra was.

"Can you tell me if she was having problems with anyone?"

"First, tell me what's going on."

I explained to Sandra as much as I felt she needed to know.

"I knew Paul had been harassing her with phone calls, emails, and sometimes dropping by uninvited," Sandra said.

"Did she let him in?"

"If she didn't, he'd be yelling outside her door and the neighbors would complain."

"Do you know if he ever hit or threatened her?"

"I never saw any bruises. Once, when I knew he was there, I knocked on her door. I thought he would leave if he saw me."

"And did he?"

"Yes, but not before he gave me a look that would make your skin crawl."

"Do you think he could have had something to do with Katie's disappearance?"

"Paul could be a real pain in the ass, but I doubt he would hurt Katie," she said, taking a sip of her wine.

"What makes you say that?"

"I've known Paul since he was living here with Katie before they separated. Once in a while he and Katie would come in for a drink. I don't profess to be an expert on human behavior, but Paul, even though he could get angry, didn't strike me as the type of person who had it in him to harm someone, let alone kill. I know that might sound naïve on my part."

It did.

"What about the guy she was seeing? What did she tell you about him?"

"I'm not sure it was serious since I don't think she wanted to get involved so soon after getting out of her marriage. And of course she knew he was married, though not at first." That was exactly what her friend Gail told me.

"It didn't bother her that he was married?"

"Obviously not."

"Is there anything more you can tell me about their relationship?"

"She didn't really talk much about him. I guess she had her reasons."

"I heard the guy she was taking tennis lessons with was interested in her. Did she mention him?"

"Just that he was a jerk. He believed he was God's gift to women. I'm sure he thought he could get any woman he wanted, but Katie wasn't interested."

"Did he bother her?"

"I think he asked her out a few times, but she always refused."

"Did she say if he got angry when she turned him down?"

"I don't recall her mentioning it."

"Do you remember the last time you spoke with her?"

"Not exactly, but when she hadn't come around for a few days, I knocked on her door, but there was no answer." She averted her gaze from mine as she spoke, and I wondered why. Then Sandra said, "I got really worried, so I went inside her apartment just to make sure nothing was wrong."

"You have her key?" I might have said it a little too harshly.

"Yes, we have each other's keys. I didn't know what to do. I had called her several times, but it went straight to voicemail. When I went into her apartment, everything looked okay, except she wasn't there. There was one small thing, but it's probably nothing."

"What is that?"

"The table in front of the couch looked crooked, like someone had moved it. As I said I doubt it's anything."

"If you were concerned, why didn't you call someone?" I said, slightly annoyed.

"I felt silly. It never dawned on me that something was wrong. Looking back, I should have known it wasn't like her not to answer my calls or leave unexpectedly."

"I have to show you something. It's a text that Mrs. Peterson got from her daughter recently. Do you think Katie wrote it?" I took out my phone to show Sandra.

"I don't know. It's possible, except…"

"Except what?"

"Why would she write that she still needed more time. I'm assuming she meant about her marriage. That doesn't make sense to me."

"Why is that?"

"Because there was no way she was getting back with Paul under any circumstances." That's interesting, I thought.

"Could it mean something else?"

"I guess it's possible. Is the guy she was involved with really dead?" Sandra hugged her arms across her chest.

"Yes. And I think Katie may have been with him at the motel."

"Oh God, this is awful. You can't think she killed him. Please, you have to find her. She could be in real danger. How come the police aren't looking into this?" Sandra got up and started pacing.

"Because at the time Katie's mother reported her missing, the police thought she left on her own, and they had no reason to think otherwise. Can you tell me if you heard any loud noises or fighting in her apartment in the days before she went missing?"

"No. If I did, I would have asked Katie about it," she said, settling back down on the couch.

"Is there anything else you can think of that might help with my investigation?"

"Not at the moment. If I do, I'll contact you."

"Can I please have Katie's key?"

After leaving Sandra, I walked next door, placed the key in the lock, and turned the knob.

CHAPTER 31

I doubt whether Sandra told me everything she knew. Most people don't. I opened the door and stepped into a small foyer. I was glad to be alone to take a careful look around. I noticed the crooked table. Maybe Katie was in a hurry and bumped into it on her way out. When I came here with Katie's mother, she never mentioned the table was moved. Her daughter was missing, so a moved table would not be foremost on her mind.

The bedroom, like the rest of the rooms, was small. The flowered bedspread gave the room some life. There were two matching dark wood nightstands with matching glass lamps. I took out the drawer from each of the tables and turned them upside down. Nothing was there. When I opened the closet door, it was full of women's clothes. I grabbed the little footstool that was on the closet floor and looked on top. There were some sweaters and other clothes stacked in plastic bags on the shelf. I reached my hand under the stack but there was nothing there.

I opened up the second closet door. Luggage was sitting on the floor along with workout weights. Standing on the footstool, I could see a cardboard box on the shelf. I took the box down and set it on the bed. Inside, it was full of photos of Katie's parents and her friends at various stages in her life. Also, there were a few pictures with her and her husband, undoubtedly captured during happier times. I closed the box and returned it to its original spot. While doing so, I noticed a manila envelope tucked away in the back of the closet. Upon opening it, I discovered Katie's passport along with some other documents, including her birth certificate. After examining the contents, I carefully place the envelope back exactly where I had found it. One thing was clear; Katie had not left the country.

There was a small desk in the corner of the room. On the top of the desk was a note reminding Katie to call the attorney. Was it a divorce attorney? If so, did her husband know she was planning on divorcing him?

I opened the drawer and in it was a bank statement showing a balance of three thousand dollars and change.

I did a thorough search of the rest of her apartment. When I opened up the medicine cabinet, I found a prescription bottle half full. I was familiar with the anxiety drug Buspirone since I had taken the same drug at various times in my life. But I was curious why she was taking it. I knocked on Sandra's door before leaving.

"Sorry to bother you again. I found anxiety medication in Katie's medicine cabinet. Would you know why Katie was taking the drug?"

"She was stressed. Between what was going on with Paul and—" Sandra stopped talking.

"What were you about to say?"

"Nothing," she said, looking down.

"Sandra, your friend is missing and she may be in trouble. If you know anything, it's important that you tell me."

"There was a teacher at her school that Katie said she was concerned about."

"What does that mean?"

"She didn't go into specifics but she thought he may have been abusing boys."

"And you didn't think that was important to tell me? Did she mention the name of this teacher?"

"I only know his first name, Gregory. She didn't want to say anything to the school since she wasn't sure, and she thought she could handle the situation herself. That's all I know. I told her she needed to tell someone but I don't think she listened to me."

"Are there any other surprises you haven't told me about?"

"No. I promise. Please find her."

I've been assuming all along that Katie was at the motel with Paul Crawford when he died. What if this teacher found out Katie was looking into him and was going to expose his secret. Was it possible Katie's disappearance had nothing to do with Paul Crawford's death?

CHAPTER 32

I knocked on three more doors before leaving Katie's building. The first person said she recently moved in and didn't know her neighbor; the second person I spoke with had no useful information. When I knocked on the third door, there was no answer, so I slipped my business card under the door.

Before going home, I stopped to pick up my usual standby for dinner: shrimp with broccoli, and an egg roll. I poured myself a glass of wine and settled in at my kitchen table with my computer. Schools usually have a website with the teachers' names listed. As I was looking through the names, there was only one teacher with the first name of Gregory. His last name was Lowell. He was a fifth-grade teacher.

From his photo, he appeared to be in his early forties, deep-set blue eyes, a thin nose, and full lips. Aside from his photo, the website had no additional information about him. My phone rang as I was stabbing at a piece of broccoli with my chopsticks.

"Isn't it kind of late for you to be calling?" I said, when I saw it was Annie.

"I was dying to know how motherhood was going."

"You're a laugh a minute. Actually, Leo is staying at Sophie's tonight."

"Already pawning him off."

"It was Sophie's idea. I had to work late, so instead of picking him up, he stayed over. I had him for one night and I think he hates me."

"I doubt that. If someone gave you a dog for a day and he stopped barking, you would blame it on yourself. You're just not used to taking care of a kid. Believe me, all you have to do is give in to whatever he wants."

"Was that supposed to be funny?" I said. Annie just laughed.

"Really, stop worrying. I'm sure you're doing fine. I doubt you'll be charged with child abuse anytime soon."

The only thing I was worried about at this moment was how I was going to find Katie Lewis.

***

In the morning I called Sophie to tell her I would be picking Leo up around 10:00 a.m. It was Saturday and I promised Leo we would be spending the day together.

I turned on my computer and coffee machine and delved into my databases to ascertain what information I could learn about Gregory Lowell. According to what I found, there was no mention of a wife or children. Lowell actually lived not too far from Katie in the West Village. Also listed was a prior address from approximately three years ago, where he had resided in Perth Amboy, New Jersey, located in Middlesex County, east-central New Jersey. I questioned why he moved. I couldn't fault him for not being married at the age of forty since Jesse was still single at the ripe old age of forty-five. Jesse was close to committing once, but realized before it was too late that he wasn't ready for marriage.

I contacted Seth and asked him to run a criminal record check on Lowell. It was a long shot since I doubted a school would hire him with a criminal record unless they were negligent and didn't bother to run a background check on him. It didn't seem likely that was the case.

When I looked at the time, I realized I was running late and ran out the door to pick up Leo.

"Maddie," Leo said when Sophie opened the door to her brownstone. "I drew a picture for you. It's you and Daddy." Sophie is an attorney for children, representing their legal interests in court proceedings, ensuring their voice is heard in matters like custody, abuse, or neglect. Besides being bright and sophisticated, she is the most self-assured person I know.

"Wow. I see, thank you." Though it was basically stick figures, he nailed my hair, straight and to my chin. Jesse and I wcrc holding hands.

"You have to put it up on your refrigerator. That's what Mommy does with all my drawings."

"I will definitely place it on the refrigerator as soon as we get home."

"Bye, Noah," Leo yelled.

"We'll see you tomorrow at Noah's birthday party. I can't believe the little guy is going to be three," I said.

"Me neither. Thankfully we made it through the terrible twos without having to give him away," Sophie said jokingly.

"What are we going to do today?" Leo asked as we got settled in the car.

"Would you like to go to the zoo and see lots of animals?"

"Does it have lions and tigers?"

"It does."

"Yeah!"

"But first I thought you could help me with something. You'll be my sidekick." Leo's face lit up. I didn't know if I should be taking Leo with me to check out where Gregory Lowell lived, but I thought what harm could it do? I wasn't planning on talking to the guy. Best case scenario, I could get a glimpse of him, maybe get a few photos.

"What do I have to do?"

"Your job is to look at everyone who comes out the front door, and if it's a man, tell me right away."

"I can do that," he said proudly, puffing out his little chest.

I crammed into a parking spot across from Gregory Lowell's three-story brick apartment building. The West Village was first settled in the 1600s. It became a stronghold for the city's bohemian community in the 1900s. It is known for its tree-lined streets, historic brownstones, and cozy cafés. Some of its notable residents are folk singer Bobby Dylan, poet Dylan Thomas, and writer Jack Kerouac. Jesse and I come down here often to walk around and get a bite to eat in one of the many wonderful cafés. I got out my cell phone.

"Okay, Leo, are you ready?"

"You got it, Maddie. Are we getting out of the car?"

"No. We have to stay inside so no one will see us." I told Leo to sit in the back so he could watch out the window.

"Wow, this is super cool. I can't wait to tell my friends at school."

I was second guessing whether this was a good idea. I was more concerned that if he mentioned it to his mother, she would think I had put his life in danger.

Fifteen minutes later, I could tell Leo was getting antsy. I tried to explain to him that sometimes what I do takes a lot of patience. It's not as much fun as it looks on television.

"I see a man," he shouted.

"That's great, Leo, but…" As I was about to say it was the wrong person, I noticed someone approaching the building who appeared to be my subject, accompanied by a boy who looked to be around eight or nine years old. The boy's shoulders were slightly hunched. I took a few snapshots and watched as they walked into his building.

CHAPTER 33

My heart was beating a little quicker. Then I thought maybe he had a son that I didn't know about. I really wanted to stay but I knew it wasn't fair to Leo.

"Hey, how about we stop to get something to eat before we head up to the zoo?"

"Did we get him?"

"We did. Good job."

Before heading to the Bronx Zoo, we stopped at a diner where we both ordered French toast. I couldn't seem to get the picture of Lowell with this boy out of my head. Was he doing something to this kid right now? I had to let it go, at least for the time being, or it would drive me crazy.

Once I stopped obsessing about what may be happening back in Lowell's apartment, I focused on having a good time with Leo. We bought food for the animals because Leo thought they might be hungry. We must have seen every animal in the place while Leo chatted a mile a minute, both to me and the animals.

We were both pretty tired by the time we left. We stopped at a pizza place near my building and ordered a pie to go. When I dished out a few spoonfuls of salad on his plate, I think Leo was too exhausted to argue with me.

***

The following day we spent at Noah's birthday party. The bike was a big hit, at least with Noah. I had noticed Cousin Will giving me the evil eye, perhaps thinking that Noah might destroy the furniture while riding the bike in the house.

Monday morning I dropped Leo off at Sophie's and grabbed a buttered bagel and coffee before heading to the office.

I spent most of the morning trying to obtain additional information on Gregory Lowell. Searching through the internet, there wasn't much. I was hoping to get a better sense of the man before confronting him.

While waiting at the school, I was listening to a Bruce Springsteen song when my phone buzzed.

"Hey, handsome. I might have to hang up quickly since I'm waiting for my subject outside a school."

"Good news! I'll be back tonight. The plane lands at 6:10 p.m., and I'll take an Uber to your place."

"Why don't I pick you up? I think Leo would enjoy going to the airport to meet you."

"How is he?"

"We both survived. We'll talk later. Love you."

"Can't wait to see you."

Five minutes later, I noticed Gregory Lowell coming out of the school talking to a woman wearing a black leather jacket over gray slacks. She was almost as tall as Lowell, about 5 feet 10 inches tall with auburn-colored hair. I quickly locked my car door and followed them on foot, allowing at least half a block between us. Two blocks later, the woman crossed the street, going in a different direction. I continued following Lowell until he reached his street and then caught up to him.

"Excuse me, are you Gregory Lowell?" Lowell looked taller than when I first saw him at his apartment building. He was wearing brown slacks and a white shirt under a black V-neck sweater. He looked exactly like his photo.

"And who are you?"

"My name's Maddie Landon. I'm a private investigator looking into the disappearance of a teacher at your school, Katie Lewis," I said, handing him my card. "Can we speak for a few minutes?"

"Sure, there's a café right around the corner. We can talk there."

After ordering two cappuccinos from the barista, we sat at a corner table in the back.

"I didn't know Katie was missing. I was told she was away for a few days."

"Do you remember who told you that?"

"I don't. It must have been one of the other teachers."

"How well do you know Ms. Lewis?"

"We speak regularly at school, but our conversations mainly revolve around teaching."

"So nothing personal?"

"Not really."

"I thought that since you live so close to Katie, you two might be more friendly."

"No. I guess we walk in different circles."

"To tell you the truth, I'm looking into someone she was having an affair with. I think something has happened to her." I was trying to gauge his reaction. If he was involved in Katie's disappearance, his face didn't show it.

"I hope you're wrong. We all think the world of her."

"I admire teachers. It can't be an easy job. Do you have a family?"

"No, never been married. Maybe one day."

"You must like kids to be a teacher."

"I enjoy teaching and I tutor kids whenever I can."

"Well, if you think of anything else, please contact me." We shook hands and I left.

There was no point in confronting him with what Sandra had told me. I didn't have enough information, and if he knew I might suspect him of being a pedophile, he would have shut me down right away. I had to find out the name of the kid that Gregory Lowell was with.

CHAPTER 34

I walked back to my car. Before starting the engine, I realized something was bothering me, but I couldn't put my finger on it. What began as a missing person case could now involve a possible pedophile. I had no choice but to look into Gregory Lowell, whether he had anything to do with Katie's disappearance or not.

I thought since I had a little time to kill before I picked up Leo from Sophie's, I'd make a couple of phone calls from my car. First call was to Paige, the teacher I spoke with at Katie's school. She might know who this kid is.

"Hello."

"Paige, this is Maddie Landon. We spoke last week regarding Katie Lewis."

"Of course. Any news about Katie?"

"Not yet, though I have a favor to ask of you. I have a photo of a young boy who I believe attends your school. I was wondering if you knew his name?"

"I'm not sure I can give you that information even if I knew who he was. I think you need to tell me why."

"Unfortunately, I can't. You just have to trust me." I didn't want her to know that I was looking into a teacher she works with since I had no proof yet.

"Is this boy in trouble?"

"No, I promise."

"Send it to me and I'll think about it."

I sent the photo of the kid. Now I had to wait.

My next call was to Katie's best friend, Gail Davis. I was curious as to whether Katie said anything about Gregory Lowell to her.

"Gail, this is Maddie Landon."

"I was planning on calling you tomorrow since I hadn't heard from you. I'm really worried about Katie, and I think something is definitely wrong."

"I'm still investigating and that's the reason for my call. Did Katie ever mention a teacher at her school by the name of Gregory Lowell?"

"No, why?" she said tentatively.

"It seems as if she had reason to believe he might be abusing kids."

"You mean a pedophile?"

"At this point I'm not sure, but she did mention it to her next-door neighbor, and she may have confronted this person."

"So he could have had something to do with her disappearance?"

"I'm still looking into other suspects. It's all speculation at this point."

"Do you think something bad has happened to her?"

"Until I learn otherwise, I'm going to assume she's alive and you should too."

"Please, as soon as you know something. I'm trying to keep positive but it's hard."

"I'll keep in touch."

So, it appears the only person she had told was Sandra. Who the hell was this kid?

***

It was almost 5:00 p.m. by the time I picked up Leo and drove to the airport. Leo was excited he was going to see Jesse. I didn't blame him, I was too. We waited with all the other cars lined up at the arrival area. The plane had landed on time.

"There's Daddy," Leo said, pointing to Jesse.

"Hey, bud," Jesse said as Leo leaped into his arms. "How's my main little man?"

When he put Leo down, he pulled me close and kissed me hard on the mouth. Driving back, I was content to keep quiet and listen to Leo as he chatted a mile a minute about all his adventures in New York.

"How about we go out for dinner," Jesse said. In unison, Leo and I both gave a big YEAH!

Wanting to score brownie points with Leo, and against my better judgment, I asked him what he would like to eat. It was a resounding Chinese. Jesse and I both smiled. We went to the Chinese restaurant in my neighborhood that knew me all too well. We let Leo pick out one dish. It was spareribs. I thought it was a good choice.

After putting Leo to bed, which was no minor matter, Jesse and I had a chance to catch up. We were lying in bed, with the door closed, wrapped in each other's arms.

"Tell me what happened in Chicago."

"It was a bust. I never found his partner. For all I knew, he could be buried in a ditch somewhere."

"So what does that mean for the client?"

"I'll do some more digging here. Maybe he'll show up. If not, we can still mount a defense, but we'll have to explore other options."

"Sounds like you have your work cut out for you. When is Karen coming back?"

"Hopefully, no later than Friday. In the meantime, Mrs. Weinstein will take care of Leo when he gets off the school bus."

"Thank heavens for her."

"Should I ask how everything went here?"

"Maybe it's the work we do. It's too unpredictable. I can't imagine being a single mother, having a job that doesn't have regular nine-to-five hours, and taking care of a kid."

"I agree. Without having a support system, it must be tough being a single parent. At least Karen had her mother before Karen decided to come back to Connecticut with Leo. Though she should have told me about Leo when she found out she was pregnant, I'm grateful she finally did."

"In answer to your question, the good news is Leo and I didn't kill each other."

"It wasn't Leo I was worried about," Jesse said, grinning. "But there is something I want to talk to you about."

I think my heart skipped several beats.

CHAPTER 35

At that moment, there was a soft knock at the door. "Daddy, can I come in?"

Jesse got out of bed and opened the door. "Hey, buddy, what's the matter?"

"Can I sleep on the floor in Maddie's room?"

"Why don't we get you back to bed on the sofa or you can sleep in your sleeping bag."

"But Maddie lets me sleep on the floor in her room." Jesse looked at me. I just shrugged my shoulders.

"Okay, go get your sleeping bag."

Leo had perfect timing and I was so grateful. Though I wasn't positive what Jesse wanted to talk about, I knew whatever it was, I wasn't quite ready to deal with it. When we were sure Leo was fast asleep, as quietly as we could, we reached for each other. At some point we pulled the covers over our heads to stifle the sounds coming from my mouth.

***

I woke up first. Both Jesse and Leo were still fast asleep. I quickly showered and put on the coffee machine. As I was looking in the refrigerator, I felt Jesse's strong arms wrap around my waist. I turned and he kissed me, first gently and then harder on the lips.

"Unless you plan on carrying this further, I think we better stop before I jump your bones. I wouldn't want to traumatize your kid any more than I already have.

Speaking of the devil," I said, as Leo walked into the kitchen, yawning.

"I'm hungry, Daddy. Maddie eats Cheerios like I do. Right, Maddie?"

"That's true. It's been my cereal of choice since I was your age."

"Wow, that's a really long time."

"If you think I'm old, then your daddy is ancient." Jesse pretended to be hurt.

After packing up Leo's stuff, I drove them to the Hertz rental place. Before getting into the car, Leo surprised me as he wrapped his little hands around my waist, giving me a hug. I looked up at Jesse as I hugged Leo back. "Drive safe. See you soon, Leo." I kissed Jesse and waved goodbye as they left. Leo's hug caught me off guard. Maybe my birth father was right when he said that kids have a way of worming their way into your heart.

"Hey, I'll meet you at The Dead Poet later if you're free," I said to Annie when she picked up.

"Six o'clock," Annie said.

I still hadn't heard back from Paige, and I was worried she wouldn't call me. For all I knew, Gregory Lowell could be tutoring this kid, though that would give Lowell the perfect pretense to take advantage of him.

Along with Paul Lewis, Jake Miller, the tennis instructor, was on the top of my list of possible suspects.

The internet revealed that at one time Miller wanted to be a professional tennis player but never made it out of the qualifiers. Training so hard for all those years and unable to make the professional tour must have been a real blow to his ego. The phone interrupted my reading. I saw it was Paige.

"Paige, thank you for getting back to me."

"I've thought about it, and unless I know what's going on and feel comfortable with your response, I won't give you the boy's name."

I was in a bind, but the more I thought about it, Paige might be an asset to me. "During the course of looking into Katie's disappearance, I spoke to a friend of hers who told me Katie was concerned that one of the teachers in your school was abusing boys."

"Are you sure?" she said, as if it couldn't be possible.

"No, without speaking to Katie, I have no idea what she knew."

"How did you get a photo of this boy?"

"I saw him entering the teacher's apartment building with the teacher."

"Maybe he was tutoring him."

"Perhaps, but what if Katie confronted him with her suspicions. If he was abusing this boy, what would he do knowing he had a lot to lose? Also, it turns out that both Katie and this teacher live just a few blocks apart."

"I can't believe this. She never said anything to me."

"Most likely she didn't want to involve you."

"What will you do if I tell you this boy's name?"

"Until I investigate this further, I'll keep it to myself for the time being."

"Is there any way I can help? If I knew who the teacher was, at least I could be aware in case I saw anything unusual," Paige said.

"If there's any truth to what Katie told her friend, it might be dangerous if he found out you had an inkling of what was going on."

"I can take care of myself. I promise you I won't approach him in any way."

"If I tell you, you need to keep this strictly confidential. That means you can't tell anyone, even a friend. If what Katie thought turned out to be false and someone in the school got wind of it, it could ruin this teacher, and that's the last thing I want to happen. Do you understand what I'm saying?"

"Yes. I promise. If I happen to see anything weird going on, I'll call you."

"Tell me the boy's name," I said.

"It's Oliver Seaver."

"What do you know about the kid?"

"He comes from a single-parent home. No father, at least that I know of."

A kid who would be susceptible to an older, authority figure, who pays attention to him.

"How do you know so much?"

"He's in my fourth-grade class. So you see why I can be your eyes and ears."

"What else can you tell me about this kid?"

"He's quiet, average student, tries hard, keeps to himself."

"The teacher's name is Gregory Lowell. Do you know anything about him?" I said.

"Not much. I believe he came here from another school about three years ago, though I'm not quite sure about the time period. To tell you the truth, I find it hard to believe it's him. Gregory is a well-respected teacher and thought very highly of. He is always the first to volunteer if we have any projects going on. Are you sure it's him?"

"According to the name I was given, it's him. Do you by chance know what school he taught at?"

"No. I'm sure it's in his personnel file but I wouldn't be privy to it."

Even if I knew the name of the school, I doubt whether they would be willing to give me any information.

When I hung up, I saw I had an email from Seth at the NYPD. There was no criminal record on file for Lowell. It didn't necessarily mean he hasn't been abusing kids, it just might mean he hasn't been caught yet.

CHAPTER 36

When I arrived at The Dead Poet, Annie was already seated at a table. The waitress came over right away and we both ordered red wine and a few appetizers.

"Annie, I don't know how parents do it. I was with Leo for a few days and I was exhausted. I felt like I had to entertain him or I was a bad person."

"You only feel that way because he's not your kid. You think most parents just sit around entertaining their kid? I don't think so."

"Well, I have a new appreciation for parents. Though I hate to admit it, I would rather be working than taking care of a kid."

"That's because the only person you ever had to take care of was yourself."

"Maybe that's selfish, but I like my freedom."

"Not everyone is cut out to be a mother. There's no shame in that. Now tell me what's going on with Jesse."

"I haven't had a chance to talk with him yet. I intended to speak him last night, but Leo had other plans and slept in my room."

"Saved by the boy."

"I will this weekend. I'm just not sure what to say."

"I know you want to live with Jesse. You're just afraid all your baggage will drive him away. I don't think you give Jesse enough credit. He knows all your stuff, and if he's willing to take a chance, you should as well."

"Do you give your divorce clients counseling also?"

"Are you kidding. That's half my job." I laughed out loud.

"Are you making any progress with the investigation?" Annie said, as she nibbled on a buffalo wing.

"My missing person case may have just taken another direction." I filled Annie in on what I had recently learned.

"That's interesting. If Lowell is abusing boys, it still doesn't mean he's involved in Katie's disappearance."

"I know. It's gotten really complicated. In the morning, I'm heading to New Jersey, where he used to live, hoping someone will talk to me. I wish I knew why Katie was concerned about this guy. It would make my life a whole lot easier."

"How's the husband looking?"

"I can't rule him out, but I don't have a strong feeling that he's involved. It seems that the tennis instructor had a fixation on some of the women at the club, including Katie. At some point I'm going to have to take another run at him."

"I have some news."

"Can it be? Am I going to be an aunt?"

"First of all, NO! Secondly, you're jumping the gun." I gave Annie my best pout I could muster up.

"Matt and I have hired an associate."

"That's the news?"

"Well, sorry my life isn't as exciting as yours," Annie said light-heartedly.

"I was just hoping, well, you know—Mazel Tov! I'm so happy that the practice is doing well."

"Yeah, me too. Let's order another glass of wine to celebrate."

After polishing off one more glass of wine and scoffing down the rest of the appetizers, we hailed a cab, dropping Annie off first.

I was lying in bed, half listening to the TV, when I remembered I never received a call back from Jake Miller. I fell asleep wondering why.

CHAPTER 37

The ride out to Perth Amboy in the morning was uneventful. I had my coffee and Lady Gaga to keep me company. Without traffic, I made it to Lowell's prior address in an hour and twenty-five minutes.

The street Lowell had lived on was lined with two-family brick houses on both sides. It seemed like a nice family neighborhood with kids playing outside; girls jumping rope. I was more of a tomboy, hanging around with the boys on my block. According to Google, Perth Amboy is a charming town rich in history, featuring an array of historical buildings, a picturesque waterfront, and a lovely park.

I knocked on the door. The woman standing before me wore black sweatpants and a matching sweatshirt, her reddish-brown hair swept up in a bun, as she held a dish towel in her hand. She appeared to be around forty.

"Can I help you?"

"Sorry to bother you. My name's Maddie Landon," I said, handing her my card.

"I'm Deborah. What does a private investigator want with me?" she said humorously.

"I'm trying to get information on someone I believe lived at this address a few years ago. His name is Gregory Lowell. Do you think we can talk inside?"

"I guess it would be alright," she said. She led me into the kitchen, which appeared to have been recently remodeled with all new stainless-steel appliances, a laminated wood floor, and a backsplash of gray and white subway tiles. We sat down at a square antique wooden table.

"Why are you asking about Gregory?" Calling him by his first name revealed to me it may have been more than a landlord/tenant relationship.

"His name came up regarding a case I'm working on in New York. I'm looking into the disappearance of a woman who works at the same school as Mr. Lowell."

"I'm still not sure why Mr. Lowell has anything to do with your case." I had to tread carefully.

"I was informed that Mr. Lowell and my missing person knew each other. While I doubt that he had anything to do with her disappearance, I'm speaking with everyone who knew her, along with her connections."

"I can't imagine Gregory being involved."

"Did Mr. Lowell rent from you?"

"Yes. He was here for a little over two years." Up close I noticed Deborah wore quite a bit of makeup. I probably use too little; blush for my cheeks and on special occasions, lipstick.

"Do you know why he left?"

"He was offered a better teaching position in New York." I doubt that was true, but that's what he probably told her.

"What can you tell me about Mr. Lowell?"

"Everybody loved him, including my two children. I'm divorced, and Gregory was always very helpful if I needed something done around the house." *I bet he was.*

"How old are your children, if I may ask?"

"Jennifer is thirteen and Charlie is ten. You know I'm feeling a little uncomfortable with all these questions. I think you'd better leave now."

I probably blew it, asking too soon about her kids.

"Well, I appreciate your time. By the way, what school did he teach at?"

"Robert Hall Elementary."

"Thank you."

Deborah seemed very protective of Lowell. Was it likely they were sleeping together? But what bothered me was his relationship with her children, especially her son. If Lowell wanted to get close to Charlie, what better way to do it than by getting close to the mother. That's how predators work. She would most likely trust Lowell to be around her children, maybe even be alone with them. I was hoping I was wrong, but I doubted that I was. Should I have mentioned my concerns to Deborah? I wasn't sure if she would have believed me. Also, if there was a possibility she was still in contact with Lowell, I didn't want to say anything that might lead her to believe Lowell was the target of my investigation.

When I got into the car, I Googled Robert Hall Elementary School. According to Google maps, it was about a mile and a half from where I was. I didn't think I would get much from the school, but nothing ventured, nothing gained.

***

I found the administration office and went inside.

"Hello, can I help you?" she said, as she got up and walked over to me. I noticed the nameplate on her desk said Marjorie Cooper. From the age spots on her hands,

Ms. Cooper was most likely in her seventies, though her face was still lovely, with high cheekbones and a smooth complexion. I could visualize a younger Marjorie Cooper. I bet she was a very handsome woman.

"My name's Maddie Landon. I'm a private investigator," I said, handing her my card. "I would like to speak with the principal if he or she is available."

"What is this about?"

"I'm working on a missing person case in New York, and the name Gregory Lowell came up. I was told he used to teach at this school."

"Let me see if Principal Thornton is available. Give me a second."

A moment later, the principal came out.

"Miss Landon, I'm Principal Thornton. How can I help you?" The fact that we didn't go into his office was a pretty clear indication this was going to be a very brief affair. From his stiff posture to his three-piece gray striped suit with a yellow and blue bow tie, I pegged Mr. Thornton for an uptight man who never broke the rules.

"Can you tell me why Mr. Lowell left your school?"

"That information is confidential."

"Were there circumstances involved in his leaving?"

"As I just said, that information is confidential. Good day."

I gave it a shot. I wasn't going to get anything from him even if their parting was mutual.

I left the town of Perth Amboy with the growing suspicion that Mr. Lowell did not leave Robert Hall Elementary of his own free will.

CHAPTER 38

Instead of going straight back to the office, I headed to Jake Miller's apartment, which was located on the West Side on Amsterdam Avenue in the fifties. He was avoiding my phone call and I wanted to know why. After riding around for about ten minutes, I finally snagged a parking spot about two blocks from his apartment building. The area where he lived was populated with high-rise buildings and local restaurants.

There was no answer when I tried the buzzer to his apartment. What now? It was almost 5:30 p.m. I thought I would wait a little while longer before going home. There was a small deli across the street where I sat and had a coffee. My phone was vibrating.

"Hey, how's it going?" I said to Jesse.

"I'm on my way to pick up Leo from Mrs. Weinstein. Then off to the pizza place in town. What are you up to?"

"Didn't have much luck when I went to Lowell's old address. The woman he rented from was pretty tight-lipped. I think something was going on between them. She also has a ten-year-old boy. What are the chances he was ever alone with Lowell?"

"Let's hope not if he is abusing boys."

"I didn't get anything from the principal at the school. He was an uptight asshole."

"I know you, Maddie, and you're not going to let this go, but your main priority is finding out what happened to Katie."

"If he's molesting kids, I can't look the other way. Besides the fact that Lowell might have something to do with Katie's disappearance. Wait, I gotta go. I'll call you later."

I dashed out in hopes of catching Jake Miller as he was about to enter his apartment building. "Jake," I yelled, trying to get his attention.

"What are you doing here?" he said, as he opened the front door.

"Why haven't you returned my call?" I asked as I stepped onto the elevator with some trepidation.

"I've been busy. I guess I forgot."

"I need a few minutes of your time."

"Sure, as long as it's only a few minutes."

I was completely surprised when I entered Jake's apartment. The hardwood floors were covered with beautiful woven area rugs. It was basically one large room with a separate kitchen. The furniture was completely modern, with a black leather sofa and a rectangular glass coffee table. There were two chrome and white leather seats opposite the couch. The walls were furnished with colorful artwork, and I noticed an alcove where Jake had a studio bed and TV. I sat on one of the chairs while Jake sat on the couch.

"I heard you paid special attention to Katie Lewis during the group lessons." I decided not to beat around the bush.

"Who told you that?"

"Is it true?"

"Even if it was, why is that your concern?"

"Because she's missing, and I know you were interested in her."

"I'll play along. Let's say I was. Do you automatically assume that anyone who pays attention to her was involved in her disappearance?"

I ignored his question. "Did you offer her free tennis lessons? And how would that work?"

"When I'm on my own time, I can do what I want." I had no idea whether he was telling me the truth.

"Did you offer free tennis lessons to your other female clients?"

"I'm not sure that's any of your business."

"Did you ask her out?"

"I may have, but she told me she was going through a rough patch and wasn't dating."

"She told you that?"

"Yes, and I respected her wishes." This guy is really smooth.

"Isn't there some sort of rule about dating your clients?"

"Would you like to check our tennis club manual?" he said sarcastically. I let that comment pass.

"What about Terri Hartley?" I noticed a momentary frozen expression, but he recovered quickly.

"What about her?"

"You went out with her, and when she wouldn't go on a second date, you became infuriated. You called her names. Insulted her. Why would you do that?"

"Is that what that crazy bitch told you? She was a tease. She was all over me at dinner, and then when I asked her out again, she refused. Does that sound normal to you?"

"You know what I think; you wanted to go out with Katie but she rejected you. Did that make you mad? Did you want to hurt her?"

"I've heard enough. Get the hell out of here."

"I'm going, but if I find out you had anything to do with Katie's disappearance, you'll regret it."

"Is that a threat?"

"Take it any way you want."

Walking down the nine flights of stairs, I thought about my interaction with Jake. I certainly could have handled that better. I should have eased into the interview, but something about him irked me. If he was in any way involved in what happened to Katie and he thought I was on to him, maybe he would make a mistake and that might cost him.

CHAPTER 39

As soon as I got in, I changed, poured myself a glass of wine, and called Jesse back.

"I just got Leo into the bath. What was the rush before?"

"I wanted to catch up with the tennis instructor before he got into his apartment."

"How did it go?"

"I tried to rattle him, but not sure if I accomplished my mission. Time will tell. How's Leo doing?"

"I think he was disappointed that he had to go back to school. According to his incessant chattering, his time with you was a hit."

"I doubt it was me, more likely his time with Noah and Marla. By the way, Leo saw some guy with green and purple hair and started giggling. I think the city will be a great addition to his worldly education."

"I'm glad you have an interest in Leo's well-being," Jesse said playfully. "By the way, Karen should be back on Thursday."

"Daddy, I'm ready to come out. Is that Maddie? Hi, Maddie," he shouted.

"Hi, Leo. See you soon," I shouted back. "I'll let you go, babe. Love you."

"Love you."

***

I went for an early run in the morning before going into the office. As I was walking down the steps to enter the brownstone where my office is located, someone from behind grabbed my arm hard. I turned and was staring into the face of Gregory Lowell.

"Who the hell do you think you are going behind my back, asking questions about me? And why is a private investigator up in my business?"

Lowell's landlord must have called him as soon as I left. Shit, just what I didn't want. I should've known from our conversation that she would contact Lowell about my visit.

"First of all, get your hands off of me. Why don't we take this inside?"

"I have nothing to say to you."

"Are you sure? I think Katie Lewis might think differently." His eyebrows shot up.

"What does she have to do with this?"

"I think you know. Did she find out your secret and threaten to expose you? Do you still want to have this discussion outside for everyone to hear?"

"Stay out of my business or you'll be sorry," he said, and he turned and walked away.

Well, I'm certainly not winning any popularity contests lately, and I'm no closer to finding out what happened to Katie.

I went into my office and turned on the coffee maker, hoping the coffee would give me a jolt of inspiration.

I began searching various social media sites since I was interested if Lowell had an online presence and was posting anywhere. I was coming up empty. Maybe he was active on sites where pedophiles talk to each other.

Unfortunately, I had no clue where to find these sites, but I knew someone who might.

"Harry, it's Maddie," I said when he picked up.

"Maddie, nice to hear from you. I was just talking about you to a friend of mine who's an attorney. I gave him your info in case he needs your services."

"Thanks, I appreciate it." I was introduced to Harry when I first became a private investigator. Harry is a whiz when it comes to finding out stuff on the computer. "How is business?"

"Chugging along. And you?"

"That's why I'm calling. I need your services."

I gave Harry Lowell's name and what he needed to search for.

"I'll give it a shot and get back to you."

I was interested in what Lowell did in his spare time besides tutoring. Around 2:00 p.m., I drove to Lowell's school and found a parking spot about two blocks away and waited near the school until I saw him come out. He was walking in the direction of his building. A few seconds later I followed on foot and kept a safe distance. He went into his apartment building and I waited at the end of his block, not knowing whether this was a waste of time or not.

About forty-five minutes later, he exited his building where he had changed from his sports jacket and slacks that he wore to school, to a windbreaker, polo shirt, and beige khakis. He walked about six blocks to a field where boys were playing soccer. I lagged behind observing him from an angle where he couldn't see me. He was sitting on the top bench watching along with the other adults, taking photos of the kids with his cell phone. Were some of the boys who were playing soccer from his school? Was that why he was watching, or was he taking photos for another reason? About a half-hour later, Lowell got up and walked toward the fence and caught the eye of one of the boys. Lowell waved and the kid nodded. He did not appear to be happy to see Lowell. I quickly snapped a photo of the boy, curious who he was. Instead of following Lowell, I decided to stay. If this kid's parents were here, maybe I could approach them.

When the game ended, the boy walked slowly with his head down toward someone calling to him. I watched as the woman seemed to be admonishing the boy. She continued ranting as they were walking. When I caught up to them, I could smell the liquor on her breath. If I was a betting woman, I would say the paper bag she was holding in her hand had something in it besides water.

"Excuse me," I said. "Sorry to impose on you. My name's Maddie, and I was asking around; I was told your son is being tutored by Gregory Lowell."

"Why is that your business?" she said in a nasty tone.

"I'm interested in having my son tutored, so I thought I would ask your son for his opinion of Mr. Lowell."

"I don't want you asking my son any questions. Come on, Tommy, let's go," she said, as she grabbed him by the arm and left.

I felt bad for Tommy. I couldn't imagine what his home life was like. Tommy, like Oliver, was the perfect kid for a predator to take advantage of, someone who would cling to anyone for attention. I had to find a way to speak with him.

My phone buzzed as I was walking toward my car. It was a number I didn't recognize.

"Hello."

"Is this Maddie Landon?"

"Yes," I said slowly.

"This is Marjorie Cooper from Robert Hall Elementary School."

"Of course I remember," I said, though I was surprised to hear from her.

"I heard what Principal Thornton said to you. I've been the school secretary for more years than I care to remember, and I know almost everything that goes on here. I'm so tired of things being swept under the rug. There was a complaint from the parents of one of the boys here, and though there was no way to know if what the boy said was true, the principal thought it best that Mr. Lowell leave."

"Do you know what it was about?"

"The rumor was that Lowell had touched him on his genitals. It appears that the boy was in the locker room getting ready for gym class when he fell and scraped his knee. Lowell happened to be there and helped him get washed up. The principal didn't know if the boy was mistaken, but because the parents were making a big deal of it, Principal Thornton thought it was best if Lowell left the school. I guess Lowell could have fought the charges but decided against it."

"Was it reported to the authorities?"

"No. Before this incident, there were no other accusations against him. Since it could have been accidental, all the parties thought it was best to keep it quiet, but the principal did not want Mr. Lowell teaching at the school anymore."

"That's interesting. Did you get any vibes whether anyone thought the kid was believable?"

"That I don't know, but please make sure my name is kept out of this."

"I promise, and I really appreciate the information. Thank you."

"You're welcome. If what Mr. Lowell did to this kid was true, I hope you find a way to prove it."

"By the way, would you happen to know where Mr. Lowell taught before he came to your school?"

"I don't."

"Well, thank you again."

I sat in my car thinking about what Marjorie Cooper had just told me and what I could do with the information. People like Lowell are very manipulative, and their victims are usually either too embarrassed or possibly threatened so they don't come forward. I believed Lowell was a predator, but how was I going to prove it?

CHAPTER 40

The next two days I tailed Jake Miller as he left work. On the first day, he walked straight back to his apartment. On the second day, I noticed when he left work, he got into a black SUV. I took note of the license plate number and followed him at a safe distance. We were definitely not going back to his apartment. About forty minutes later he stopped in front of a small, single-family ranch in Astoria, Queens. He parked in the driveway and grabbed a couple of brown paper bags from the backseat that appeared to be filled with groceries. He let himself in with a key, stayed for about an hour, and left. Whose house was this? I took some photos and wrote down the address. Why would Jake have a house in this area? The homes on the block were most likely built in the fifties for middle-income families. But ever since the area became gentrified with loads of ethnic restaurants, vintage shopping, and modern art galleries, it attracted younger people to the community. Still, something was wrong with this picture.

I followed him back into the city where we parted ways. I was tired and it was late. Though I was curious whose house Miller had gone into, it would have to wait till the morning.

***

I dragged myself out of bed the next day, took a quick shower, and filled a mug to the top with a new brand of coffee I had bought. I sat down at the kitchen counter and turned on my laptop. Searching his license plate number through the New York State Department of Motor Vehicles, it listed that the black SUV was registered to a Jason Miller. I guess he likes going by the name of Jake. The age matched. The address listed was the one on Amsterdam Avenue. Next, I did a property search with the address I had for the house in Astoria, Queens. It was owned by a Sheila Gray. Who the hell was Sheila Gray?

I picked up my car from my garage and drove back to the address in Astoria. I knocked on Sheila Gray's door, but there was no answer. The same results with the next two doors. As I was about to knock on a fourth door, I noticed a woman across the street coming out of her house.

"Excuse me," I shouted, as the woman was opening her car door. "Hi, sorry to bother you," I said, as I caught up to her. "I'm looking for Sheila Gray. She lives in that house," I continued, pointing to Sheila's house. "She doesn't appear to be home." The woman gave out a hearty laugh.

"If she opened that door, I would pee my pants." She must have seen the quizzical look on my face. "Oh, honey, she's dead."

The woman looked like a throwback from the sixties. She was maybe in her fifties. Her blonde hair was piled high on top of her head, and she was wearing black liquid eyeliner on both her upper and lower eyelids with blue eyeshadow. I detected a slight Southern accent.

"How long ago did she die?"

"About two years ago. Why are you lookin' for her, hon?"

"It's regarding an insurance policy."

"Maybe her son can help you. Though he's rarely here, for the past month or so I've seen him a few times."

"Did you notice if he was with anyone?"

"I don't think so. Why are you asking?"

I had to think fast. "The company that hired me to investigate wasn't sure if he was single or married. Maybe it has something to do with the insurance policy." Though what I said probably didn't make sense, I doubt she would realize it.

"By the way, I'm Maddie Landon," I said, handing her my card.

"I'm Joyce McClosky." Joyce was certainly jovial. I bet if I engaged her in conversation, she would chew my ear off. "If I see him, should I tell him to call you?"

"No, I'll catch up to him where he works, but thank you. Oh, by the way, Sheila Gray has a different last name than her son. Do you know why that is?"

"Jake is Sheila's stepson. Her husband, Mike Gray, died about five years back."

"Thank you."

If he only comes by infrequently, why would he bring all those groceries to the house?

After Joyce McClosky drove away, I quickly walked to the back of Shelia Gray's house, looking in all directions, making sure no one had eyes on me. There was a sliding glass door that led into the living room. I pushed on the handle but it was locked. I peeked in. The furniture looked as old as the house, with plastic covers on both a green couch and a red and beige striped club chair. The wall-to-wall green carpeting, from what I could see, looked worn. It didn't appear that anyone was living here. I moved on to the side of the house. There was one window that was boarded up from the inside, most likely a basement window. There was no side door that led into the house. On the other side was a window that overlooks a bedroom. I tried pushing it open from the bottom but it was locked from the inside. Without having any proof that Miller had anything to do with Katie's disappearance, I decided not to break in, at least for now.

With his mother deceased, why was he holding on to the house? He could get a couple hundred thousand for it. So why keep it?

CHAPTER 41

Driving back to the city, it was bothering me that Katie hadn't told anyone what she found out about Lowell. If it was just a hunch with no incriminating evidence, why say anything at all to her neighbor Sandra? There had to be more to it. Did Lowell find out she was onto him and threatened Katie?

"Hi, Harry," I said when I saw it was him calling. "Give me some good news."

"There's a site called 'The Dark Horse.' It's where like-minded people find each other. He's on it, but the way they exchange information and ideas, unless you're part of their group, you wouldn't pick up on the meaning behind their words. Unfortunately, there isn't anything illegal in what they're doing."

"Shit, did you find anything else?"

"No. He most likely keeps a low profile since he's a teacher and wants to stay under the radar."

"Thanks, Harry. Send me your bill."

"Take care, Maddie."

Rather than heading back to the office, I decided to see if I could catch Tommy, the boy I had seen at the soccer game, as he was leaving school. I arrived just in time to see the students as they were coming out. I spotted Tommy walking by himself.

"Tommy!" He turned and saw me. He looked at me for a moment and then I saw the recognition on his face.

"My mother says I can't talk to you."

"I want to help you. I'm a private investigator. My name's Maddie Landon. What's your last name, Tommy?"

"Jenkins," he said in a whisper.

"Nice to meet you, Tommy Jenkins. What grade are you in?"

"Please, I can't talk to you. Go away."

"I will, but I have a feeling that Mr. Lowell might be hurting you."

"Please, leave me alone." Tears were slowly running down his cheeks.

"Okay, but I want you to take my card. If you need to talk, call me anytime. Will you do that?" He nodded and quickly walked away.

Tommy didn't have to tell me what Lowell was doing to him. His eyes told me everything.

I was only a few blocks from Katie's apartment building. Was it possible Katie had some evidence that could prove Lowell was a pedophile? I still had the key Sandra had given me. It was worth another look.

I searched the whole apartment again, but I was coming up empty. Could I be wrong and there was no evidence? Maybe whatever she found out was on her phone. If there was proof, could she have hidden it somewhere else? But where?

"Mrs. Peterson, it's Maddie Landon."

"Any news?"

"I'm working on a couple of possible leads. I have to ask you a question. Do you remember the last time Katie was in your home?"

"Why is that important?"

"Please, do you remember?"

"I have to think. It was maybe a couple of months ago. Like I told you, we weren't getting along recently."

"Is it possible she could have come in when you weren't there?"

"I guess. She did have a key. But why would she?"

"I'm not sure. I'll be there in about an hour if that's alright with you?"

"I'll be here. Do you know where Katie is?"

"Not yet. I'll see you soon." And with that, I hung up.

"What is this all about?" Mrs. Peterson said when she let me in. "Please tell me what's going on." Mrs. Peterson had on another hideous outfit. This time it was a beige pantsuit that made her already pale complexion look paler. I had to tell her something.

"Right now it's just a hunch. If Katie wanted to hide something, I'm thinking it wouldn't be at her place; maybe she would hide it here. That's all I can tell you now. I promise as soon as I know anything more, you'll be the first to know."

"Why would she want to hide something? If what you're saying is true, that means Katie might be in danger."

"I know this is difficult, but let's not get ahead of ourselves."

"Katie still has her old room. Maybe it's up there."

"Thank you."

I followed Mrs. Peterson up the stairs and into Katie's room.

"This might take a little while." I was trying to be subtle. I didn't want Mrs. Peterson watching me.

"I'll just be downstairs if you need me," Mrs. Peterson said, though she paused before leaving, seemingly reluctant to go. She looked so sad as I watched her leave the room. I couldn't dwell on it since I needed to remain focused.

I began my search in the obvious places, starting with the nightstand drawers. I pulled them out and turned them over, hoping to uncover something hidden. The desk drawer contained the usual assortment of items: pencils, pens, and a stapler. I glided my hand beneath the desk, but there wasn't anything there. The closet revealed only a few old clothes hanging. I lifted the mattress, but again, there was nothing.

Feeling frustrated, I sat down on the desk chair, just staring into the room. If I was hiding something, where would I place it? I walked over to the bed and got down on my knees, sliding my hand across the underneath. Nothing. I went to the other side of the bed and slid my body partially in. My hand felt something small, attached with tape. I pulled it off. It was a thumb drive. My heart skipped a beat.

Mrs. Peterson was waiting for me at the bottom of the stairs.

"Did you find what you were looking for?"

"No." At this point I had no idea what was on it. Until I knew, I had no reason to share what I found.

"Why don't we sit for a moment." We went into the kitchen and sat down at a round white table with blue and white cushions on each of the four chairs. The room had a homey feel to it.

"I've been looking into one of the teachers at Katie's school. She may have found out something about this person that they didn't want anyone else to know about."

"You think he hurt Katie?" she said with an anxious look on her face.

"I don't know. I'm trying to find out more about him. Before I know what I'm dealing with, I would rather wait and see what develops. For all I know, this person has nothing to do with Katie's disappearance."

"Are there any other leads?"

"There are, but again, until I know more, I'd rather not get your hopes up."

"Please just find her. It's been a nightmare. I can't sleep. The only thing on my mind is Katie. I pray she's safe somewhere. You have to find her."

I didn't know what to say, so I kept silent.

CHAPTER 42

On the way back to the office, I was uneasy about what I was going to find on the thumb drive. Why would Katie suspect Lowell of abusing a boy unless she witnessed something?

I realized I hadn't eaten all day. I picked up a sandwich at the deli before heading in. I settled at my desk, turned on my computer, and inserted the thumb drive. It contained six photos. One showed Lowell at a boys' softball game, taking photos of the kids. Another was of a young boy, about eight or nine, entering Lowell's apartment building with Lowell—I recognized Tommy. The next photo captured Tommy coming out of the building, and though it was hard to tell, he appeared to be crying. The last two photos were of Oliver, the boy I had originally seen with Lowell. They were sitting on a park bench, Lowell's hand resting on Oliver's knee while Oliver looked down. Unfortunately, none of these images provided the damning evidence I needed. I required more concrete proof.

"Hey, Jesse, give me a ring." Two seconds later my phone rang.

"Sorry, I was just hanging up from another call. What's going on?"

I caught Jesse up to speed. "It's a good thing he isn't standing in front of me. I'd kill him."

"Maybe it's not what it seems."

"You really believe that?"

"No, but I also don't want you doing anything crazy."

"If I confront him, he's just going to give me a cock-and-bull story. What is my alternative? If I was still on the police force, I would have the guy's sorry ass sitting in front of me sweating."

"I understand how you feel, but you have to be careful. At this point, you don't have enough evidence. Keep digging."

"What about approaching the parents of one of the boys? They might be willing to talk with me," I said.

"I think it might be too soon. I doubt they're going to believe you. What about the tennis instructor? What do you think is going on with him?" Jesse said.

"I have no idea. But doesn't it seem really weird about the groceries if he's not living there?"

"Is it possible someone else is staying in the house?"

"Maybe, but the woman across the street didn't mention seeing anyone else there."

"Listen, I'm just pulling into Mrs. Weinstein's apartment to pick up Leo. Karen is coming back tomorrow, so I'll see you on Saturday. I'll come down there. Be careful."

"Tell Leo I said hi."

"Will do. Love you."

I was looking forward to having the whole weekend with Jesse, just the two of us, but I wasn't looking forward to the conversation I needed to have with him.

CHAPTER 43

I intended to confront Lowell before I went to the parents of the two boys. I wanted to give him a chance to hear his side of the story. Though the photos were compromising, they weren't proof that Lowell was doing anything to these boys. Would he want to talk to me after the scene outside my office? Instead of ambushing him at his place, I could try calling him and making nice. I picked up my phone and dialed his number.

"Hello," he said cautiously.

"Mr. Lowell, it's Maddie Landon. Please don't hang up on me. I want to sincerely apologize if I came on too strong when you caught me off guard outside of my office. I'm just trying to find out what happened to Katie. Do you think we can talk somewhere?"

I could almost hear the wheels turning in his head. How was he going to play it? If he was smart, he would hear what I had to say.

"I can stop by your office in about an hour."

"Great. I'll see you soon."

***

Gregory Lowell was seated in my office. From the look on his face, I knew he was only here to try and win me over. He didn't know the extent of what I suspected.

"I'm sorry if I accused you of any wrongdoing a few days ago. I was out of line. According to your landlord in Perth Amboy, you were a perfect tenant. I'm interested in why you left and came to New York."

"I'm originally from New York and the opportunity at this school came up. I thought it was a good move."

I decided not to antagonize Lowell and bring up what Marjorie Cooper told me about why he was asked to leave his last school.

"Do you have any idea why Katie mentioned your name in a conversation with a friend?"

"I don't. The last time I spoke with Katie, she asked me about one of the boys I was tutoring. She had seen him coming out of my building and she questioned why he was being tutored at my place."

"And what did you tell her?"

"It's complicated. Oliver comes from a single-parent home, and his mother works all kinds of crazy hours. I thought instead of tutoring him at his apartment or at the school, he would feel more comfortable in a different environment. Oliver needs a male figure in his life. Besides tutoring him, I've been teaching him how to play chess; sometimes we go to the park and hang out." Well, that was real smooth. It was time to play a little hardball.

"And what about Tommy Jenkins?"

"What about him?"

"You're also tutoring him." I could see by the surprise look on Lowell's face, he wasn't expecting Tommy's name to come up.

"Ms. Landon, I tutor kids. I'm not sure what you're getting at."

Tread lightly, Maddie.

"Do you have any idea why Tommy was crying after leaving your apartment?"

"Who told you that?" he said, trying to keep his temper in check.

"It doesn't matter. Can you tell me why?"

"How would I know?"

"I think you do know. Was he upset about something that happened at your place?"

"This is ridiculous. I have no idea what you're talking about, and I have no idea where Katie is," he said, as he got up abruptly to leave.

"You might want to see these." I placed the six photos on my desk.

"Where the hell did you get these? They don't prove anything." Was it rage or fear that I saw in his eyes?

"Do you want to know what I found out? You think the principal here might be interested in why you were asked to leave your last school? Did you kill Katie because she confronted you with her suspicions about what you did to those boys?"

"Go to hell," he said, and stormed out of my office.

Well, if he didn't know I was on to him, he did now. I hope he wakes up every morning sweating, wondering if I plan on telling the principal what I knew. But I was still clueless whether he was involved in Katie's disappearance, and that worried me.

***

The next morning I went for an early run. When I got back, I looked up the name Miriam Seaver in my databases. It was an uncommon name, and fortunately there was only one. I remember Paige telling me that Oliver lived with his mother and there was no father in the picture. It listed her age as thirty-four. I wrote down the address and took the train down to where Miriam Seaver lived. As I reached her apartment building, I rang the intercom buzzer.

"Who is it?" she said with concern.

"Ms. Seaver, my name's Maddie Landon. I'm a private investigator, and I need to speak with you about Oliver."

"Is my son alright?" I could hear the worry in her voice.

"Yes, he's fine, I promise." I hoped my reassurance would ease her anxiety. Moments later, the buzzer sounded and I entered the building. I found my way to the staircase, and as I climbed up to the fifth floor, I thought about what I might say to Ms. Seaver.

The door opened to a frazzled-looking woman, her brown hair hastily tied in a ponytail, though several strands had escaped, hanging loose. She wore a wrinkled shirt and baggy slacks.

"Are you with the school?" she asked, her voice tense.

"No. If I could come in and explain." I handed her my card.

"Excuse the mess," she said, glancing around as she moved the stuff from the couch to the floor. "I didn't have a chance to clean up yet."

"That's fine. You must be very busy working and taking care of your son." I gave her a warm smile, hoping to put her at ease.

Despite her disheveled appearance, her eyes were sharp and focused, looking at me for answers.

"Please explain what this is about?" she urged, settling into a rattan chair with a white cushion. I sat down on a brown covered couch that had clearly seen better days, its fabric worn and faded.

I took a moment to gather my thoughts, aware of the weight of the conversation I was about to have.

"I'm looking into the disappearance of a teacher at Oliver's school. In the course of my investigation, I noticed a young boy, who I later found out was your son, entering an apartment building with a male teacher from his school."

"Oh, that's Mr. Lowell. He's tutoring Oliver. Why is this any of your concern?" she said, nervously fidgeting with her hands.

"Can I ask why Oliver is being tutored at Mr. Lowell's apartment instead of at the school or here for that matter?"

"Well, not that it's any of your business, but Mr. Lowell is like a big brother to Oliver. I have to work a lot and he spends time with him, especially on the weekends when I'm at my job. It's good for Oliver to have a male figure to look up to."

I was trying to choose my words carefully, but there was no way to broach the subject easily.

"Have you noticed any changes in Oliver lately?"

"What do you mean?" she said, clearly annoyed at what I had just asked.

Without any real proof, I was trying to avoid accusing Lowell of sexual abuse.

"My only interest is in your son's well-being. Have you noticed any changes in Oliver's behavior lately? They could be subtle changes, and it would be understandable if you ignored them since they could be attributable to many things."

"What are you getting at?" Ms. Seaver said, raising her voice.

"Please, just ask your son if anything has been upsetting him and gauge his reaction."

"I think you should leave now," she said sharply.

"I will, and I'm sorry if I've upset you in any way."

It was a long shot. My only hope was that I had put some doubt in Ms. Seaver's mind and she would talk to her son. My frustration was mounting. I had no proof that either Lowell or Jake Miller had anything to do with Katie's disappearance. I had to do something, and fast, before my investigation went to hell.

CHAPTER 44

I heard the familiar knock on my door Saturday morning.

"Breakfast first or me?" I said, as soon as Jesse walked through the door.

He looked as if he was thinking about it for a quick second, and then threw me over his shoulder, walking into the bedroom and gently dropping me on my bed.

Later, as we were wrapped in each other's arms, Jesse stroking my hair, I looked into his big, dark brown eyes and knew it was now or never.

"I have to tell you something, but I don't want you to interrupt me until I'm finished."

"Okay, shoot."

"I'm not sure if you noticed, but I felt anxious while we were looking at apartments. To be honest, even though I agreed to move in together, I'm really scared. It's not about you—I know you'd make a fantastic partner. My worry stems from my own issues; I fear that you might end up resenting me, and I couldn't bear that. While I genuinely want to live with you, I also want to ensure you don't wake up one day feeling resentful. Okay, I'm done. You can speak now."

"First of all, I did notice, and I was going to broach the subject with you when Leo interrupted us. I'm flattered that you would think I would make a great partner, but you give me too much credit. I'm not the perfect person you think I am. I have stuff too. We all do. I haven't made it to the ripe old age of forty-five without some issues of my own. Why do you think I've never married. I like my independence, but since I met you, even though you're stubborn, you can be a real pain in the ass, and I have to walk up and down stairs with you because you won't get into an elevator, you make me happy."

"You say that now, but…"

"Listen to me. If I'm willing to accept you as you are, you have no reason to deny me that pleasure. If there are any problems, we just need to get them out in the open. You can't be afraid to tell me what's on your mind. If you're not willing to do that, then you're right, we shouldn't live together."

I was so moved by what Jesse said, the only words that came out of my mouth were, "I'm famished, let's eat."

We spent most of the day indoors, enjoying each other's company. The only time we ventured out was to pick up some ingredients for Jesse to prepare a delicious dinner. One definite perk of living with Jesse is that he would be doing most of the cooking—after all, he wouldn't want to starve.

***

On Sunday morning while we were eating breakfast, the phone rang.

"Ms. Landon, it's Miriam Seaver. I don't know what to do," she said, sounding almost hysterical. "I asked Oliver about Mr. Lowell. At first he told me nothing was wrong, but when I kept asking him questions, he started crying and locked himself in the bathroom. He won't tell me what's wrong and he won't come out. Please come over. I need your help."

"I'll be there shortly. Try to remain calm."

"We have to go. I'll explain everything on the way."

When Ms. Seaver let us in, I introduced her to Jesse.

"Let me talk to Oliver. Maybe I can get through to him," I said to Ms. Seaver.

"Oliver, my name's Maddie. I'm here to help you. Please open the door so we can talk, just the two of us. If you're not ready to talk, that's okay; maybe you can at least listen. I saw you coming out of Mr. Lowell's building, and you looked so sad. Do you think you can tell me what happened?" A moment later, the door opened, and I went inside and closed the door behind me.

When I came out, Oliver went into his room and I spoke to Ms. Seaver.

"Before I tell you what Oliver said, can you explain what prompted him to lock himself in the bathroom?"

"I knew Oliver was quieter than usual in the past few weeks. When you were here the other day and asked me if Oliver was acting differently lately, I didn't say anything to you. I was ashamed because I've been so consumed with keeping everything together, I didn't see what was going on with Oliver. I guess I was worried you would judge me.

"This morning I decided to talk to Oliver. I asked him if anything was wrong, but he said no. I could tell by how upset he got that something wasn't right. So I asked him again if anything was bothering him, and that's when he ran into the bathroom."

"You have no reason to feel guilty. You thought you were doing what was right for your son. You couldn't have known what was going on."

"Do you think he hurt Oliver? I'll never forgive myself if he did. Please tell me what Oliver said to you?"

Her eyes looked desperate. I knew I wasn't going to tell Ms. Seaver everything her son told me.

"Please, let's sit down," I said gently, gesturing toward the couch. I took a quick glance at Jesse, gauging his reaction as I began to speak.

"I need you to understand that Oliver is very confused and upset right now. He needs someone he can talk to about what's happened to him. Mr. Lowell has been taking advantage of him, and Oliver was threatened not to tell anyone. I don't want to go into all the details at this moment, but it's important that Oliver sees a doctor. You also need to go to the police and report that your son has been sexually abused. In the meantime, please refrain from contacting Lowell, no matter how much you might want to. And I would advise against asking Oliver any more questions; he's already in a fragile state."

I was having a hard time looking at Ms. Seaver. I can't imagine what she was feeling.

"How can he do that to my son? I trusted him. If he was here right now, I'd kill him," she said, screaming, tears running down her face.

I wanted to make it better, but I knew there wasn't anything I could say or do that would.

"Why don't you take Ms. Seaver to the police station now and I'll stay with Oliver," Jesse said.

"Just let me change. Thank you so much, Maddie. I'm not sure I could handle this alone."

"What did Oliver tell you?" Jesse said when Miriam went into the bedroom to change.

"He took pictures of Oliver naked. He clammed up when I asked him about the photos."

On the way over to the police station, I told Miriam I had been a detective with the NYPD, and knew the name of someone there that we might be able to speak with. Ms. Seaver kept crying and blaming herself. When we arrived at the precinct, I asked to speak with Detective Brian Griffin. Luckily, I was informed he was still working there.

"Maddie Landon, good to see you," he said, extending his hand to me when he came to greet us. I introduced Brian to Ms. Seaver. Brian was Irish through and through. He was tall and carried some bulk. His eyes always had a twinkle in them. "This doesn't appear to be a social visit."

"Unfortunately not." We went into Detective Griffin's office. It was as I remembered—cramped, a metal desk and chair, and file cabinets against the wall. I let Ms. Seaver tell Detective Griffin what she knew, which wasn't very much.

After asking Miriam several questions, he told her they were going to set up an appointment for a therapist to speak with Oliver.

"Are you going to talk with Gregory Lowell?" Ms. Seaver asked.

"Yes. We'll bring him in for questioning."

"Miriam, do you mind waiting at the front for me. I need to speak with Detective Griffin on another matter."

When Miriam left, I told Brian that, according to Miriam's son, Lowell had taken nude photos of him. I explained that I was investigating Lowell as a possible suspect in my missing person case, and could he ask Mr. Lowell some questions in connection with Katie's disappearance to get his perspective. I decided to hold off on mentioning Tommy Jenkins until I had a chance to speak with his mother again.

Miriam was very quiet when we left the precinct. I realized it was a lot for her to deal with. After dropping Miriam back at her apartment, I couldn't help but wonder how Gregory Lowell would react when the police contacted him.

CHAPTER 45

"Are you okay?" Jesse said on the ride back from Miriam Seaver's apartment.

"This kid will never be normal again. Lowell robbed him of his childhood and maybe his life."

We were stopped at a light when a blue sedan sped through the intersection, crashing into a car approaching from the right. The sound of the crash was horrific.

I opened the car door, barely hearing Jesse as he was shouting for me to wait. I ran as fast as I could. When I got to the crash, there was a woman trapped inside on the driver's side. I banged on the window. "Help is coming! Remain calm!" She was pleading with me, her eyes glazed over in a blank stare. Drenched in my own sweat, it was hard for me to see. When I looked again, the person staring back was that twelve-year-old girl trapped, crying for her parents. I was clawing at the window. The next thing I knew, someone was pulling me back.

"You're safe now, Maddie," Jesse gently said, holding me as my body racked with sobs. "The ambulance is on its way. They'll take care of her and get her out. She's going to be just fine."

"I have to wait until they pull her out. I can't leave."

I watched as the firefighters and paramedics arrived. When they were finally able to remove her from the car, she looked at me as if to say, "Thank you." I took her hand for one brief moment, watching as tears were slowly falling down her face. After the ambulance left, we walked back to the car.

"I saw myself in the car screaming. It was terrifying. How could that happen?"

"For that moment you may have been reliving the night of your parents' car crash. It may not be that unusual," Jesse said, clasping his hands over mine. "Seeing that woman trapped and the stress from the past couple of days could have brought it on."

"It felt so real. This isn't the first time I've relived that night. It's happened before, but never as intense. You sure you still want to take me on?"

"I do," Jesse said, and we both laughed, realizing the pun.

"It's after 2:00 p.m. I'm starving," Jesse said. "How about I treat my favorite lady to a nice lunch and a glass of wine?"

"I won't put up any argument."

"You're quiet," Jesse said as we were eating. "A penny for your thoughts."

"It was a case I was involved in when I was on the police force. This seven-year-old boy was being abused by his stepfather and the mother was in denial. The only reason we found out about it was because a neighbor was suspicious of the guy. The neighbor noticed bruises on the boy, but when he asked the kid what happened, the boy clammed up. The neighbor said he recognized the signs of child abuse from his own nephew. We went to the house to talk to the mother and she kept saying nothing was wrong. She said that her son was accident-prone when we mentioned the bruises. There wasn't anything we could do. A week later, the kid was dead."

"That must have been rough. It's hard to imagine that people like that exist."

"The mother knew yet she wouldn't say anything. I don't understand it."

"Who knows; she could have been damaged herself. Maybe she was abused growing up. It's hard to say. The weird thing is, she probably loved her son."

Though neither of us brought up what happened earlier, I was worried. I didn't want to mention to Jesse that the incident might have been triggered by our decision to move in together. After my parents' accident, the thought of being trapped extended to my relationships, leading to a feeling of being smothered. I know it's not rational, but sometimes those feelings rear their ugly heads.

***

When Jesse left in the morning, I sent Detective Griffin the photos Katie had taken, plus the two I took of Oliver and Lowell.

"Ms. Seaver, it's Maddie. I was checking to see how you and Oliver are doing."

"I didn't send Oliver to school today and thankfully, I had the day off. Oliver has an appointment to see the court-appointed therapist at her office later. What do you think she's going to ask Oliver?"

"I'm not sure but they're trained to talk to kids. It'll be fine."

"What about afterwards. How is he going to get through this?"

"I would strongly suggest Oliver gets professional help."

"But how am I going to afford it?"

"We'll figure out a way. There are places that work on a sliding scale. Did Detective Griffin mention if Lowell had been in for questioning yet?"

"He said he was being questioned today."

Did that mean they asked him to come in on his own, or they picked him up at his apartment?

"This is all my fault," Miriam said. "When I met Mr. Lowell, he was so nice and seemed so caring. He was sympathetic to the fact that Oliver didn't have a father. He told me he knew from his own childhood growing up without a father what impact it could have on a child. I practically gave Oliver to this man. How can I be so stupid?"

"Predators know how to manipulate people. He knew you were vulnerable and acted on it."

"Every time I look at Oliver my heart breaks."

"Things will get better. Please call me if you need anything, or want to talk, day or night."

If Lowell was angry enough, would he try and come after me? I slipped my gun into my ankle holster and left my apartment.

CHAPTER 46

The air was cold, or maybe it was the way I was feeling. I couldn't help but think about Gregory Lowell and where he was now. Was he sitting in one of the interrogation rooms at the police station? I wish I knew what was going on. I heard a buzzing sound and realized it was coming from my phone in my backpack. I quickly retrieved it.

"Hello." It was a number I didn't recognize.

"Is this Maddie Landon?"

"Yes. Who is this?"

"It's Joyce McClosky. We met a few days ago and you had asked me about Sheila Gray. I saw her son yesterday and spoke with him."

Now my interest was piqued.

"I told him that someone had been looking for him. I hope that was alright."

Oh shit. "What did he say?"

"At first I thought he was upset, but then he just smiled."

"Is that it?"

"Well, not exactly. I asked him if anyone was living in the house, and he gave me a strange look, as if he had no idea why I would ask him that. After a moment of silence, he explained that he was stocking the place with food since he was thinking of moving in for a few weeks."

That's interesting. I wonder if there was more to the story than he was letting on.

"Then he said goodbye quickly and went inside. I hope I didn't say anything I wasn't supposed to?"

"Oh no, don't worry about it. Thank you for calling me."

He must have figured out by now that I've been following him. If he had anything to do with Katie's disappearance, he would be watching his back. Should I be worried that he might be watching me?

I drove to my office and was lucky enough to find a spot only two blocks away. Waiting for me was a ton of administrative paperwork that I'd been ignoring for the past couple of weeks, including two reports I had to write up for clients. One report involved a witness I had to find for an upcoming trial, and the other was for a husband who was way behind on his alimony and support payments, and was nowhere to be found. I was lucky enough that someone I spoke to ratted the guy out.

By the time I finished, it was dark out. I was surprised how empty the streets were as I walked to my car. I thought I heard a noise behind me, but when I quickly turned, no one was there. Maybe I was getting the jitters knowing both Gregory Lowell and Jake Miller were out there, and I was a possible threat to them.

"Excuse me," someone said, tapping me on the shoulder from behind. I nearly jumped out of my skin.

"I'm sorry if I scared you. I noticed as you were about to get into your car that your rear passenger tire is flat." The guy was big, maybe 6'3" and scruffy looking. His clothes were crumpled. I don't think his shaggy beard had seen a comb or scissors in months.

As soon as my heart stopped thumping, I thanked the guy. "You saved me from riding on a perfectly good tire."

"Sorry to disappoint you, but it looks like your tire was slashed."

"Shit! Really!" I looked closely and the guy was right.

"If you have a spare, I can help you with that."

"I really appreciate it, but that's why I have Triple A."

"It might be a while before they come. I can do it."

My suspicious nature wondered if this guy had an angle; and was he homeless or just had bad grooming? Since he was probably right about when Triple A would show up, I warily said, "I'll let you change the tire but only if I can pay you."

"How about a hundred bucks?"

"Only kidding," he said, when he saw the bewildered look on my face.

In fifteen minutes, my spare tire was on the car. "Listen, can I buy you a cup of coffee or something."

"There's a coffee shop around the corner. Would you mind sitting with me?"

"I really have to get going."

"Hey, I just saved you about two hours, if not more."

I couldn't argue with that. "Okay," I reluctantly said.

"My name's Lucas."

"Maddie, nice to meet you." When we were looking at the menus the waitress had handed us, I told Lucas he could order whatever he liked. He gave me an appreciative look.

"I'll have the fish special," Lucas said to the waitress. I ordered eggs and a toasted bagel.

Lucas told me he had been homeless for a little while: Bad business decisions; a terrible divorce; and years of depression. He had a kid he hadn't seen in about eight months. I could tell by the way Lucas spoke that he was well-educated, most likely in his forties but looked about a decade older.

"Strange that yours was the only tire slashed on the block. Someone out to get you?" he said, amused. But when he saw the expression on my face his look changed.

"Damn! Is someone after you? Maybe I can help."

"Why don't we change the subject." After we finished eating, I asked Lucas if I could drop him somewhere. He declined and said he would walk.

"Here's my card, Lucas. Be careful out there."

"You too and thanks for the meal," he said.

As I was getting in my car, I saw the surprised look on his face as he glanced down at my business card.

CHAPTER 47

Driving home, I thought it was interesting that Lucas had picked up on the fact that someone may have a vendetta against me, even though he said it jokingly. I was curious what business he had before his life went to shit.

"Hey, babe. I had the most intriguing interaction with some guy I just met," I said, when I saw it was Jesse calling.

"Should I be jealous?"

"Nah! You're still number one."

"Good to know. So what was so captivating about him?"

I relayed to Jesse everything that had transpired with Lucas.

"How do you know he wasn't the one who slashed your tire?"

"Why would he? He doesn't even know me."

"He may not be who he seems. Isn't it possible someone put him up to it or he had something to do with Katie's disappearance?"

"I guess, but I just didn't get that vibe from him."

"He could be manipulating you, or whoever slashed your tire has something else in store. I'm not saying that's what's going on, but if it is, then they likely know where you work and where you live. Just be careful."

"I will."

"I was hoping you might want to look at some apartments with this old geezer over the weekend. I don't want to push you, Maddie, if that's not what you want."

I couldn't help but smile. When Jesse had told me that despite all my flaws, I made him happy, I had goosebumps all over. The bottom line is that Jesse made me happy too, and right now, that's all I could ask for.

"I'd be delighted to go apartment hunting this weekend if your old body can take the stairs." I could picture the grin on his face.

* * *

The next morning I went for an early run. The morning sky was just beginning to lighten as I entered the park. I began my three-mile loop around, first starting out slowly, giving my body time to warm up; then I began running at a nice easy pace. My mind wandered to Tommy Jenkins. I didn't know if Lowell was still tutoring him, but Mrs. Jenkins needed to know what was going on. I was worried about her son. Suddenly I tripped on something and couldn't catch myself in time as I fell to the ground. Someone was running toward me, his beanie pulled low on his head.

"Hey, are you alright?"

"Yeah. Didn't see that branch."

"It probably fell off the tree. Kind of weird. Anyway, have a nice day."

Am I being paranoid thinking the branch wasn't there by accident? Jesse's words were spinning around in my head. But how could someone know I would be running exactly where that branch fell? It had to be a coincidence and not some sinister plot.

My phone rang as I was walking back to my building. "Hello."

"Maddie, it's Lucas, your knight in shining armor." I was surprised to hear from him. "I hope I'm not bothering you. I saw from your business card you're a private investigator. Listen, from the reaction on your face last night, I'm pretty sure someone is harassing you. Can we meet? There's something I have to tell you."

"I really don't have time right now. Whatever you need to say, can you please tell me over the phone?"

"I wasn't completely honest with you last night. I didn't lose my business; I was an FBI agent and got fired because I screwed up royally on a case. The truth is, I started drinking on the job and, together with my depression, well you can see how it all caught up to me."

"I'm sorry to hear that. How long have you been living on the streets?"

"Only about eight months."

"Do you get something from the government each month?"

"Yeah, but it's not much. I give most of it to my wife since she needs it—especially now that she's relying solely on her income. I want to get off the streets, but I've gotten used to this life. I have a routine, and as strange as it may seem, no one bothers me here."

"What do you want?"

"I want to help you."

I had no idea if what Lucas told me was the truth, but even if it was, I had no intention of allowing him to be part of my investigation. Though I didn't think he had anything to do with Katie's disappearance, I had to be careful.

"I know what you're thinking, but I'm an experienced investigator. I might have access to resources that could help you."

"Why would you think I need your help? Look, I'm sorry. I work alone, but I appreciate the offer."

"I can understand if you don't believe what I've told you, but you can call Jeremy Sanders. He works for the FBI and he'll vouch for me. If you do change your mind, you have my number."

When I got to my office, I turned on my computer and ran a couple of cursory searches on the internet. What I read confirmed that Lucas Stevens was telling the truth; he was an FBI agent, but beyond that, there wasn't any information about him. I didn't find that unusual considering his occupation. He might be able to help me on certain cases, but because of his current situation, I couldn't trust him. I found it interesting that he felt comfortable living as a homeless person—maybe his previous life had been too stressful for him. In a strange way, I felt a connection to this man.

CHAPTER 48

After talking to Lucas, I put in a call to Detective Griffin. I was dying to know what was going on with Lowell and if he had spoken to him about Katie.

"Detective Griffin speaking."

"Brian, it's Maddie Landon."

"You saved me a call. At this point it's an active investigation, and therefore I can't tell you much. He was smart enough to have a lawyer present so he wasn't going to incriminate himself by admitting that Katie Lewis accused him of something."

"But what about the photos Katie took?"

"You know very well he can spin them anyway he wants. But when I asked him flat out if he had anything to do with her disappearance, he vehemently denied it. That's about all I can say."

"I don't know what I was thinking. Why would he admit to hurting Katie, even if he did."

"By the way, the school did suspend him until our investigation is completed."

"Well, that's something. He has to be abusing other boys. Also, you should check into the last school he taught at."

"Maddie, we'll handle it. Please don't do anything to jeopardize our case."

"I won't," I said reluctantly.

I didn't plan on interfering with Griffin's investigation unless I somehow found out Lowell was connected to Katie's disappearance.

Just as I was about to make a fresh pot of coffee, my door opened.

"Hey, delivery," I heard from the reception area.

I wasn't expecting a delivery. I pulled my gun from my desk drawer and tucked it in the back of my jeans. I saw the long box. Maybe Jesse was sending me flowers, but that seemed out of character for him.

"Do you know who the package is from?"

"I don't."

"What flower shop are you with?"

"The PlantShed. Sign for it, please."

I did and gave the guy a five-dollar tip. I brought the box into my office and looked at it as if it was kryptonite, slowly opening it. Inside were six roses dyed black. It was vile. I pulled out the note. It read: *You are Dead.* I kept staring at it. My thoughts went to my slashed tire. Could it be the same person?

I called the number I found for the PlantShed. "Hello. I just received flowers with an anonymous note. Can you please tell me who sent flowers to Maddie Landon?"

"One moment." When they got back on the line, they said they had no record of anyone sending flowers to me. "So there was no delivery from your store to me?"

"No."

"Did anyone purchase six long-stemmed roses in the past few days?"

"Wait, let me check." When he picked up, he told me there was a receipt for six roses purchased two days ago.

"Did they pay by credit card or cash?"

"Cash." Of course! What did I expect.

"Did you take the order?"

"No, it was probably Melanie. She comes in at 2:00 p.m."

"Thanks." I thought it would be worth a trip to the shop to see if Melanie could recognize either Miller or Lowell from their photos.

When I thought about it, a flower shop wouldn't deliver roses sprayed with black dye. Whoever bought the flowers must have paid someone to deliver them. I never even looked at what I was signing. Just as I was getting ready to dump them in the garbage, my phone rang.

"You bastard. I lost my job because of you. Who the hell do you think you are spreading lies to the police. If you think you can get away with this, you're in for a rude awakening."

"Sending me dead black roses and a threatening note aren't going to scare me."

"What the hell are you talkin' about. You won't get any warning when I come after you." And then dead air. Was Lowell just playing me or was it someone else who sent the flowers?

Another call was coming in. "Hello," I said, trying to suppress the anger in my voice.

"Ms. Landon, it's Paul Lewis. I haven't heard from you and I'd like to know what's going on with the investigation."

"Mr. Lewis, I don't work for you, and therefore I don't have to tell you anything. If you had been upfront with me from the beginning, I might be more inclined to talk with you. All you've done is lied to me about your relationship with Katie and I don't like being lied to." I hung up. Maybe I could have handled it better, but everything was getting to me. And the fact that I had nothing concrete to report to Katie's parents was stressing me out.

CHAPTER 49

I locked my office door and walked outside. Winter was making its presence known, and I could feel the air changing. I zipped up my leather jacket. When I looked up at the sky, I saw large dark clouds looming over.

The PlantShed was only a fifteen-minute walk from my office. When I arrived, I saw a young woman behind the counter wrapping a bouquet of flowers for a male customer. I observed her as they were interacting. Melanie was young, maybe in her early twenties, with pitch-black, long, straight hair and a warm, light brown complexion. The smell of the flowers was making my nose itch. Maybe I was allergic. Then I saw the dog in the corner. He could be the culprit.

"Melanie," I said, when the gentleman left. "My name's Maddie Landon, and I was wondering if you could help me. I received six long-stemmed roses from someone who purchased them from your shop the other day. The person who delivered them said he was from the PlantShed, but your boss told me there was no delivery scheduled to someone with my name at my address. Unfortunately, the card wasn't signed and the person paid cash. Would you happen to remember what the person looked like?"

"We get so many people coming in. Sorry."

"I have three photos I'd like to show you. Maybe you'll recognize the person."

I handed her the photo of Lowell first, then the one of Miller I took when he was at his mother's house in Astoria, and the third of Katie's husband, Paul Lewis.

"I'm sorry. None of these guys looks familiar."

"What about height or build?"

"To tell you the truth, I just don't remember. Is it possible the flowers didn't come from our shop?"

"Perhaps. Here's my card anyway in case you remember anything."

Well, that was a bummer. On the way back, I stopped at a new coffee place that had opened recently. It was hard to imagine what the city needed was one more café, yet I stepped inside. The room was spacious, and the tables were far enough apart that you had some privacy. People had their noses stuck in their computers. If I yelled "fire," would anyone bother to look up? The three chalkboards against the wall listed everything they served. I ordered a cappuccino and a blueberry scone from the barista.

I sat down and thought about where the investigation was headed. I wasn't even sure anymore if I was on the right track. I was glad to hear Lowell was suspended from his teaching position, but I still couldn't rule him out as a suspect in Katie's disappearance. When I mentioned the flowers to Lowell, he sounded genuinely surprised. Could he be that good of an actor?

I was so distracted that I barely heard my phone.

"Ms. Landon, it's Dorothy Peterson," she said when I picked up. "A Detective Stone and another detective were just here asking me all sorts of questions about Katie that I couldn't answer. You need to come." Mrs. Peterson sounded frantic.

It was just a matter of time before Detective Stone got around to interviewing the Petersons. I was curious what Mrs. Peterson told them.

"I'll be there as soon as I can. Please don't worry."

"Tell me exactly what Detective Stone said to you," I asked her when we were seated in her living room. I noticed Mrs. Peterson's hands shook slightly as she moved aside a book that was on the chair before she sat down.

"He wanted to know about Katie's relationship with the guy who died. I told him I had no idea. I'm not sure he believed me," she said with a worried look.

"Why didn't you tell him about their affair?"

"I panicked. I was afraid they might think Katie had something to do with his death. They said he was killed at the motel. This is terrible. They wanted to know what you told us."

Thankfully, I never mentioned that Katie may have been in the motel room when Crawford was killed.

"What did you tell them?"

"That you were looking for our daughter, and you never mentioned anything about what happened to the guy at the motel."

"What you said is true. The detectives were just fishing."

"But I didn't tell them about the affair," she said, her expression filled with unease.

"It's okay. I had told Detective Stone that Katie may have known Peter Crawford. I didn't mention anything about an affair."

"I wish my husband had been here. They showed up so unexpectedly, and I was so nervous."

"It's not uncommon to be nervous when being questioned by the police. It can be very intimidating."

"I need you to tell me exactly what's going on. I don't like being in the dark. This is my daughter we're talking about," she said with concern etched on her face.

"I'm not sure, but I believe Katie may have been at the motel with Peter Crawford the night he was killed."

"Oh my God! But where is she then?" I could see the fear in her eyes.

"At this point I don't want to make any assumptions."

"Do you think my daughter could have killed him?"

"I doubt that very much."

"But you don't know. You must have some thoughts about it?"

"It's possible they had an argument that turned ugly, and it was an accident, or maybe she wanted him to leave his wife and he refused. Like I said, I don't believe she killed him. I'm thinking more along the lines that someone else killed Crawford and either Katie witnessed what happened and is hiding because she's afraid or…"

"Or what? My daughter is dead!"

"I don't think that's the case. Whoever killed Crawford wouldn't have taken Katie and killed her somewhere else; her body would have been found alongside Crawford's in the motel room." I couldn't be sure that was the case, but I didn't want that thought lingering in Mrs. Peterson's mind.

"You're no closer to finding my daughter than you were two weeks ago," she said, raising her voice.

"Actually, that's not true. I have two possible suspects. I know it's hard to trust me right now, but I believe I'm getting closer to finding out what happened to Katie. I need a little more time."

Mrs. Peterson was silent. What choice did she have. The police weren't even looking for her daughter.

"The moment you know something, I want to know."

"That's a promise."

Though I realize how upset Mrs. Peterson must be, I hate being put under the microscope. People don't understand that these things take time. Maybe they watch too many television shows where the villain is caught in an hour. It's hard to compete with that.

Though I told Mrs. Peterson I was close to finding Katie, the truth is, I wasn't so sure. I went back to my office to think.

CHAPTER 50

I poured myself a cup of coffee and sat with my feet up on my desk, staring at the ceiling. Okay, Landon, let's start with what we know to be true.

First the husband: Paul Lewis stalked his wife and a former girlfriend. He wanted to get back with Katie but she wanted no part of him. Could he have followed Katie and Peter Crawford to the motel? If he did kill Crawford and Katie saw him, what happened to Katie?

Jake Miller: We know he liked Katie and paid special attention to her at the tennis club. He asked her out but she refused. Terri Hartley told me that Jake was extremely angry when she turned down a second date with him. When Terri returned home to her apartment, she saw Miller standing outside looking up at her window. It freaked her out. Could Miller have followed Katie and Crawford to the motel? If he did, what happened to Katie?

Gregory Lowell: We know that Katie was concerned that Lowell might be abusing boys at her school. We don't know if she confronted Lowell. If she did, why would Lowell kill Peter Crawford? Why not just kill Katie?

Though Paul Lewis stalked his wife and wanted her back, would he harm her if he found out she was having an affair? According to her neighbor Sandra, she didn't think Lewis was a killer. I still had my reservations. Jake Miller may very well be a psychopath. If he saw Crawford as an obstacle to getting Katie, he could have killed

Crawford. But the question still remains, where is Katie? The phone interrupted my thoughts.

"Is this Maddie Landon?"

"Yes. How can I help you?"

"My name's Dean Wycoff. You slipped your card under my door a few days ago. Sorry I'm just getting back to you, but I've been busy. What is this about?"

"One of your neighbors, Katie Lewis, is missing, and I was canvassing your floor to see if anyone might have some information about her."

"Unfortunately, I really don't know her, just in passing."

"What about her husband; did you know him at all?"

"I'm sad to admit that I wouldn't recognize him if I tripped over him." It's unfortunate, but I can't entirely fault him. I hardly know my neighbors myself; in fact, I'm not even sure I know their first names. I suppose I haven't been the best neighbor either.

"But is it possible you might have seen something, but didn't think anything of it at the time?"

"Give me a second. Well, a few weeks ago I bumped into a guy coming out of her apartment carrying something. Not sure what it was."

"Why was that unusual? It could have been her husband."

"I just thought it was a little weird since he was in such a hurry and never even made eye contact."

"Can you describe him?"

"Not really. He had on one of those beanie hats that covered part of his face."

"Can you give me a more definite time period?"

"Maybe three weeks ago. That's the best I can say."

"If I send you three photos, would you be able to recognize him?"

"I doubt it, but let's give it a try."

I sent Dean Wycoff a photo of each of my suspects. I wasn't holding my breath that he'd be able to identify any of them.

"Ms. Landon, unfortunately, it's just too hard to tell. There is one thing I can tell you, the guy I bumped into had some sort of ring on his left hand where you would normally have a marriage band. I'm not sure if that helps."

"It does. Any idea what kind of ring it was?"

"Sorry."

"Thank you, and if you happen to think of anything else, please call me."

I wasn't sure if Paul Lewis still wore his wedding band. Miller and Lowell weren't married, but I couldn't remember if they wore a ring on their wedding finger. Still, it was a piece of information that could be invaluable.

Shit, I forgot to call the realtor. My therapist would say I didn't forget, it was my subconscious repressing the thought. She would probably be right. I might as well do it now before it slips my mind again.

"Sarah, it's Maddie Landon, how are you?"

"I'm fine. I was going to call you. I have a few apartments I thought you might want to look at."

"Any chance something else opened up in my building?"

"Actually, the people who signed the contract are having some difficulty getting a mortgage. I'm not exactly sure what the problem is, but if it should fall through, I'll let you know. In the meantime, do you want me to set up some appointments for this weekend?"

"Yes, that would be great."

"I'll call you when I have a better idea of the time."

I just remembered that I was going to call Paige. She answered on the first ring.

"Paige, it's Maddie Landon. How are you?"

"I heard Lowell was suspended. What happened?"

"I can't get into all the details, but there's an open investigation since Oliver Seaver's mother went to the police and accused Lowell of abusing her son."

"Wow, Katie was right. Poor Oliver."

"There's another boy in your school, Tommy Jenkins. I'm pretty sure Lowell has been sexually abusing him, too. I tried speaking to his mother at a soccer game; not the most friendly person, and I could smell liquor on her breath."

"I'm not surprised. Other parents have complained about her when they run into her at school or at the soccer games."

"I need to know where she lives. Would you happen to know her first name?"

"It's Marilyn. If you need her address, I can get it for you in the morning."

"Thanks, but I'm pretty sure I can find it."

"I still can't believe it. He was so nice and seemed to genuinely care about the kids."

"That's what they want you to believe. You can never tell. Thanks, Paige."

I found Marilyn Jenkins' address in two minutes. I wrote it down and planned on going over to her place at some point tomorrow.

I locked up and was walking to my car, thinking about Katie Lewis, when suddenly I felt a hand on my shoulder. My heart racing, I quickly turned around, only to see Lucas standing in front of me.

"What the hell, are you trying to give me a heart attack. This is the second time you practically scared me to death."

"Sorry, Maddie. I was trying to catch up to you."

"How about, 'Hey, Maddie, wait up.'"

"I'll remember that for the next time. I thought I'd walk you to your car, just to make sure everything's alright."

"You don't have to do that, Lucas. I can take care of myself."

"I know. Do you have time for a cup of coffee. Maybe talk about the case."

I looked at my watch. It was already 6:30 p.m. and I was hungry. "Have you eaten yet?"

"No."

"Why don't we get some dinner. It's getting colder out. Do you have a warm jacket?"

"Yeah, but I usually only bring out the big guns when it's really cold." I couldn't help but chuckle.

We went to a burger place a few blocks from my office and sat down in one of the booths. The menu was extensive, with different variations of a burger. When did burgers become so complicated? To me a good old-fashioned burger is made with ground beef, not lamb or salmon.

I ordered a classic burger with a slice of tomato and french fries. Lucas ordered the same except with onion rings and a slice of cheddar cheese. Looking across at

Lucas, under that scruffy beard was a face that I bet was once very handsome, but now was weathered and aged from the elements and his hard lifestyle. When he smiled, which was not very often, you could envision that younger, handsome version of himself.

"So, what do you do all day long besides thinking of ways to scare me to death?" I said.

"I'm kind of the neighborhood watchdog. I make sure nothing bad is happening."

"I guess you missed the guy who slashed my tire." Lucas gave out a hearty laugh. It was nice to hear.

Our food came and we dug in.

CHAPTER 51

"Maddie, I know you don't trust me and I understand why, but sometimes another point of view can be helpful," Lucas said, as he popped a french fry in his mouth. "When I was with the Bureau, my team would meet every week and we'd brainstorm."

"Why don't we table this for a while." I was tempted to take Lucas up on his offer, but I still wasn't sure if he had a hidden agenda.

"You mentioned you have a kid," I said, wanting to change the subject.

"Max, he's eight. After the divorce, I started drinking and my ex didn't trust me with him. I don't blame her. Now that I'm sober, Max and I talk on the phone."

"Isn't that a reason to get off the streets so you can see Max?"

"Don't you think I want to see him? He means everything to me. I feel like I've failed so miserably. It seems so much easier when no one has any expectations of me; then I can't disappoint anyone."

"I understand exactly what you mean. You're not the only one whose life dealt them a raw deal. If your son means so much to you, then maybe it's worth another try. I can't imagine it's that easy living on the streets."

We ate the rest of our meal in silence. Lucas walked me to my car and I didn't give him any resistance.

"I'll see you around, Maddie."

"Thanks for keeping the neighborhood safe," I said, before starting my car. I noticed a slight upward curve around the corners of his mouth. I was glad he recognized my subtle humor.

When I got home, I poured myself a glass of wine and stood at the kitchen counter, contemplating how different my life could have turned out. Despite having wonderful parents, a part of me felt shattered when they told me that I was adopted. Even after discovering the truth about my biological parents, I realized I couldn't turn back the clock; it still remains as a thorn in my side, a constant reminder of unanswered questions that linger in my past. I finished my wine and headed straight to bed.

***

In the morning I decided it was time to confront Jake Miller. I didn't know if he had anything to do with Kate's disappearance, but he was definitely concealing something and I was curious to know what that was.

I drove over to his apartment building and waited for him to come out. I knew he wasn't expected at the tennis club until 11:00 a.m. As I was turning the channel on the radio, there was a loud bang on my window that startled me.

"Are you stalking me?" Miller shouted. "I know you've been following me. What's your problem?"

I got out of my car and stood right in his face. He backed up. "You're my problem. I know you had something to do with Katie's disappearance and I'm going to prove it."

"If you keep harassing me, I'm going to the police."

"Go ahead. I'd like to see it. By the way, what is that ring you're wearing? Is that your college ring?"

"That's none of your business," he said, walking away quickly. I was curious whether that was the ring Wycoff might have seen when he bumped into the guy outside of Katie's apartment.

***

Later in the day, I waited outside the tennis club for Jake Miller. I wanted him to see me, to know that I was watching him closely. I was certain the last thing he would do was go to the police.

As he left the club, our eyes met briefly. He stopped, and with a sneer, mouthed "fuck you," before continuing on his way. I couldn't help but hope that my presence had stirred enough anger in him to drive him into doing something reckless.

When I looked at the time, it was still early enough to go over to Marilyn Jenkins' place. I didn't care if she took my advice or not, but I intended to tell her what I knew about Gregory Lowell, and hopefully she cared enough about her son to make sure he got the help he needed.

As I approached her street, I was surprised at the area in the West Village Marilyn Jenkins lived. It was a high-income neighborhood. I rang the intercom buzzer to her apartment.

"Who is it?"

"Mrs. Jenkins, it's Maddie Landon. We met at your son's soccer game. You need to hear what I have to say and then I'll leave."

"What if I don't let you in?"

"I'll keep ringing until you do." A minute later, the buzzer to the door sounded, and I went inside. I found the stairs and walked up the five flights to Mrs. Jenkins' apartment. I knocked and the door opened.

"Say what you have to say and leave," she said, as we stood in the hallway. She must have seen the look of surprise on my face as I caught a glimpse of the living room from where I was standing. It could have been featured in *House Beautiful*.

"You're just like everyone else. What, you thought I was white trash, living in a pigsty?"

"I really don't care how much money you have or what your apartment looks like. I only care about your son. Gregory Lowell has been suspended while an investigation is pending, looking into allegations of sexual abuse. I believe your son may have been abused by Lowell. For his sake, you need to talk to him. I know you love your son and will do whatever it takes to get him the help he needs."

"You said what you came here to say, now just leave."

I left, not certain what Marilyn Jenkins was going to do. I wanted to believe she'd make the right decision.

Driving home, I thought about Tommy and what his future would look like if his mother ignored what I said. I wasn't sure if there was anything more I could do at this time.

When I got home, I quickly changed and heated up some leftovers. I kept going over and over in my head how this whole thing with Katie might have played out. Let's say Jake Miller was fixated on Katie and she rejected him, what would he do? Would he be consumed by finding a way to be with her? If he followed Katie and Peter Crawford to the motel, did he kill Crawford and grab

Katie? Was it possible that no one heard anything coming from that room? Maybe, since the person in the adjacent room said he left about 8:00 p.m. and Jake Miller didn't check into the motel until around 7:00 p.m.

If it was Jake Miller that Dean Wycoff saw coming out of Katie's apartment, why would Miller take the chance of being seen? Was it because he needed Katie's overnight bag so people would think she left for a few days? Could Katie be at the house in Astoria right now? Somehow I had to get into that house even if it meant breaking in.

***

I thought I heard the faint rattle of the front door. Maybe I was imagining it. No one can get past my doorman. I listened again, but there was only silence. I rolled over trying to get back to sleep when I heard a faint creak coming from my hallway. That wasn't my imagination. Where the hell did I put my gun? I crept out of bed, my heart pounding, chills running down my spine, looking around for something to use as a weapon, when I grabbed the book that was on my nightstand. I cautiously peeked into the hallway, but it was completely dark and eerily quiet. I took a few steps and could hear sirens whizzing by outside. I took a few more steps and then I heard it, another creak. I slowly walked toward the living room when I saw a silhouette of a person, but before I could react, he lunged at me, causing the book to fly from my hand. The hate in Jake Miller's eyes was palpable. I fought him but he was too strong. His hands wrapped around my throat, squeezing tightly. I tried screaming but no sound came out. He loosened his grip for a moment and I screamed as loud as I could and kept screaming, waking myself up, drenched in my own sweat.

My breath was coming hard and fast. When I was finally calm enough, I stripped off my white cotton T-shirt and panties and stood under the cold shower, letting the water wash over my body. Though I knew sleep was going to elude me, I lay down still feeling unsettled from the dream, but eventually dozed off, sleeping fitfully.

CHAPTER 52

My phone was ringing. Who the hell was calling me at 6:30 in the morning. "Hello," I said, my voice groggy from sleep.

"Ms. Landon, this is Detective Stone. The body of a young woman was found not too far from the Horizon Motel. I'd like you to take a look and see if this is your missing person."

I jolted up. For a moment I couldn't speak.

"Ms. Landon, are you still there?"

"Yes, sorry. You caught me off guard. Why are you asking me to identify the body? Why not her parents?"

"I'd prefer if we know for sure before we call them. I'd rather they avoid that ordeal unless it's her. I'll text you the address."

On the ride up to Yonkers, I was dreading it might be Katie. What if it did turn out that Jake Miller was the one who killed her, and I had missed the signs all along? The thought sent a chill down my spine, making me question everything I thought I knew. How could I have been so blind? What would I tell her parents? I tried to put those thoughts out of my head.

Detective Stone greeted me at the site. We were standing in front of an abandoned building.

"The body was found by some teenagers who were surely up to no good, but fortunately for us, they were the ones who discovered it. This isn't going to be pretty so prepare yourself. Apparently, the victim's body has been lying here for a few days." I was sweating, praying it wasn't her as we walked over to where the body was located. Though I had never seen Katie in person, I'd looked at her photo so many times, her face was ingrained in my mind.

The smell of decay and dampness hit me. All the windows were broken and paint was peeling everywhere. The thought of rats nipping at my legs gave me the jitters. The inside of the building was in complete disrepair, presumably from being empty for such a long period of time. I walked carefully, navigating all the debris on the floor, stepping over wooden boards with nails sticking up.

I looked down at the body. She was naked from the waist up. Beneath her short black leather skirt, her red panties hung loosely around her ankles. Her skin was pale, most likely due to the lack of blood circulation. Because she wasn't exposed to the elements, the decomposition process was slowed down. She had bite marks on her breasts and from the red marks around her neck, it appeared she had been strangled. I let out a deep breath when I realized it wasn't Katie. This woman had blonde hair and was younger than her. Also, her mother had mentioned that Katie had a butterfly tattoo on her right upper arm.

"It's not her," I said to Detective Stone, letting out a sigh of relief.

"Are you positive?"

"Absolutely."

"I'll walk you to your car," Detective Stone said. "I have a few questions for you."

Oh shit! My head was pounding. All I wanted was to get out of there and go back to sleep.

"How is your investigation going? Any luck?" Stone said.

"Nothing yet."

"I was thinking that your subject knew Peter Crawford more than just casually." I didn't say anything. "I'm thinking she may have been at the motel with him the day he was killed. What do you think?" I knew he was goading me. I wasn't going to take the bait.

"I guess it's possible, but I haven't found any evidence to that effect." Technically, it wasn't a lie. His questioning gaze told me he didn't believe me.

"I spoke to Katie Lewis's parents. They didn't have much to tell me. Either you're a lousy investigator or you're hiding something. Which is it?"

I knew he was angling for information and I had to give him something. If I told him that Crawford and Katie were having an affair, then he would want to know how I found out, and I didn't want Katie's friend involved.

"Look, I want to be helpful, but I don't know any more than what I have already told you."

"Hmm, but you went to his house looking for him."

"Yes, but only because he had crossed paths with my subject and to find out if he knew anything that could help with my investigation. Did you check into the wife? If she was aware that her husband was cheating, she might have a reason to kill him."

"Are you trying to tell me how to conduct my investigation?"

"Of course not. Look, if I find out anything that could help with your case, I'll contact you. I appreciate that you called me and not the Petersons."

I got into my car. Stone leaned in. "Keep your nose out of where it doesn't belong."

CHAPTER 53

I sped away, glad to be out of there. Though I hated seeing that poor, lifeless girl, I was just grateful it wasn't Katie lying in that abandoned building.

"Hey," I said when Jesse picked up. "I spoke to the realtor and she's setting up some appointments for us to look at apartments this weekend. She also mentioned that the people who are buying the apartment in my building might have a problem getting a mortgage."

"That's good news. Are you sure this is what you want?"

"Are you trying to talk me out of it just when I was warming up to the idea of living with this great guy I know?"

"Okay! I'm happy you're on board. How's your day going?"

"Funny you should ask." I told Jesse what transpired earlier.

"That must have been awfully stressful. You still have to go on the assumption she's still alive unless you find out otherwise."

"The more I investigate, the more I believe the tennis instructor is behind Katie's disappearance."

"I have faith you'll figure it out."

"You and Annie might be the only ones," I said.

"By the way, Leo asked me if we were going to get married. Did he say anything to you?"

"He asked me, too. I told him that each couple does what they think is best for them."

"That's quite an insightful answer."

"I have my moments."

"Yes you do."

"Any luck with your case," I asked Jesse.

"It turns out the dead guy was into gambling and owed quite a bit of money to the wrong people. I'm looking into that angle."

"Be careful. I don't think loan sharks want you snooping into their business," I said.

"I appreciate the advice."

"By the way, my friend—the guy from the street—turns out to be a former FBI agent who was fired for drinking on the job and making a mistake that had serious consequences. It's weird that in some ways he likes being homeless."

"No disrespect to this guy, but maybe he's taking the coward's way out. We know that life can be trying at times and unfair, but that's no reason to cop out."

"You may be right, but I can't help feeling this connection to him, and I'm not sure why. Does that sound crazy?"

"No, babe. I get the feeling you want to help him."

"I still don't know if I can trust him. I'm being cautious."

"Duty calls. Stay safe. I love you."

It was still early, and I knew Miller would be working until 5:00 p.m. I couldn't shake the image of the poor girl in the abandoned building. What if it was Katie, suffering at the hands of Miller? Driven by a sense of urgency, I headed to his mother's house in Astoria, Queens. I had to find out if Katie was inside that house, and there was only one way to uncover the truth.

The rain that was falling an hour ago was now coming down in full force. I could barely see the car in front of me, and it didn't help that I forgot to buy new windshield wipers. I drove slowly since the roads were slick. I finally made my way to the Major Deegan and followed the GPS directions from there. Though I told Jesse I thought Jake Miller might have had something to do with Katie's disappearance, I had no hard evidence to back it up. It could easily have been some psycho Katie picked up at a bar. Between the pounding rain and my anxiety, my hands gripped the steering wheel so tight I was losing feeling in my fingers. What if Jake Miller wasn't involved and I'd wasted all this time going after the wrong person? The truth is, I had no other suspects. I ruled out Paul Lewis and Gregory Lowell, focusing primarily on Jake Miller. Could I be wrong? It wouldn't be the first time.

My wipers were struggling to keep up with the downpour. I tried to concentrate on my driving. When I finally reached the house, though the rain was coming down in buckets, I decided to park my car around the corner where no one could see it. I pulled up the hood on my rain jacket and kept my eyes focused on my surroundings. There was no sign of Jack Miller's car or the neighbor's car from across the street. I quickly went around to the back of the house. I had my nose right up against the sliding glass door, and everything appeared the same as the last time I was here. There was no movement. I could feel the tension in my body as I contemplated what I was about to do next. I reached for the tool that was in my pocket in order to open the door. Thankfully, there wasn't a stick on the inside of the glass door to prevent it from opening. My palms were sweating as I worked to open the lock. I heard a click and I slowly slid the door open. The pounding in my chest was palpable as I stepped into the house.

CHAPTER 54

The atmosphere inside was chillingly quiet, suggesting that no one was home. I called out, "Katie, are you here?" but received no response. I began to walk around, trying to get my bearings. There was no sign that indicated Sheila Gray updated the furniture during all the years she lived here. The green rug was matted down from wear and tear, and there were bare spots on the more heavily trafficked areas. Getting a better look at the green couch, the armrests were frayed.

The master bedroom lacked a lived-in feeling; the bed, covered in a pristine white chenille bedspread, appeared untouched, as if it hadn't been slept in since the mother passed away a few years ago.

I walked into the kitchen. It was old and outdated, like the rest of the house, the brown linoleum cracked along the edges. When I opened the refrigerator, it only contained water bottles, jam, and peanut butter. The cabinet doors above the sink were stocked with canned goods, crackers, and cookies. Was he getting ready to move in as he told Mrs. McClosky? There appeared to be a door that I didn't notice at first, since a large fake plant obstructed its view. As I was pushing the plant aside, I felt something press against my nose. It was damp with an unfamiliar scent. I tried pushing it away, but the hands holding it in place were too strong; a heaviness came over me and then everything went dark.

When I woke up, I was lying on the floor of a cold, concrete basement. There was a faint smell of mildew. My hands and feet were tied, my mouth gagged, and my shoes were gone. I heard muffled sounds coming from my right. As I glanced in the corner of the room, there was a woman bound and gagged, tears running down her cheeks. In that moment I recognized her—it was Katie Lewis. A wave of relief washed over me; she was alive.

I heard a door open and footsteps slowly coming down the stairs. I was staring into the eyes of Jake Miller.

"So, you're finally awake. I'm sorry it had to come to this. I warned you, but you wouldn't listen." I tried to speak but I couldn't. I pushed myself up in a sitting position.

"I can take that gag off, but only if you promise not to scream. If you do, it's lights out again, and I don't think that's what you want. Nod if you understand."

I nodded. Miller walked over and pulled down the gag. It was a relief getting that rag out of my mouth.

"Who else knows you're here?" he asked in a harsh tone. "I'd be careful what you say. If I find out you're lying, whoever tries to come through the front door I'll shoot. Do you understand?" I nodded again.

"Good, I'm glad we got that settled. Now answer the question."

"No one. I never mentioned this place to anyone."

"Not even to your boyfriend or your friend Annie?"

How does he know about them?

"I can see by the look on your face you're surprised. You're not the only one who is capable of following someone. I also have cameras all over this place. I know you were here before and that you were talking to that nosy Mrs. McClosky. Now tell me again who knew you were coming here?”

“I’m telling you the truth. I didn’t tell anyone where I was going.”

“I don’t believe you. I’m going to ask you one more time. Who knows about this place?”

“Again, no one. I don’t know how to prove it to you.”

“You better hope you’re telling the truth because if I see anyone come near this house, it will be on your head if anything happens to them.”

“What was your plan when you took Katie? To lock her up in this basement until when?”

“My plan for Katie is none of your business. Katie and I are bonding. Isn’t that right, Katie?” Katie didn’t nod or respond in any way. She must be so frightened. I was afraid I knew what he meant when he said they were bonding. This guy was a complete psycho. How the hell was I going to get us out of here?

“Can you please take the gag off of Katie? She’s not going to scream. The poor girl is practically catatonic.”

“I didn’t realize you were in charge.”

“I’m just saying.”

“Katie is doing just fine. Right, Katie?” Again, no reaction from her.

“I’m going upstairs now. I’ll be back with dinner a little later. By the way, don’t bother trying to reach for the phone that was in your back pocket. I’m keeping it for safe storage. I’ll be right upstairs so if I hear any shouting, there will be consequences.” He pulled Katie’s gag down and left.

"Katie, I'm Maddie. Your parents hired me to find you. Are you alright? Has he hurt you?" Her eyes opened wide.

"I'm scared. I'm never getting out of here," she said, as the tears kept streaming down her face.

"We will. I promise." I had no idea how I was going to make that happen.

"Your parents are worried sick about you. They never believed you would just leave."

"Is it true nobody knows where you are?" she said frantically. I nodded.

"If no one knows we're here, how are we going to get out of here?" Her voice was trembling.

"I'll figure something out. Have you tried to get away?"

"I couldn't. He keeps me tied up when he leaves. And the window is too high up for me to reach. Besides, it's boarded up."

Oh shit!

"Did he hurt you, Katie?" I could see the fear in her eyes. I didn't ask her again. I knew what the bastard was doing to her.

"Is he feeding you?"

"Peanut butter and jelly sandwiches. Sometimes he brings food in and takes me upstairs to eat with him. But he's always careful that I'm not out of his sight."

I knew Katie was beautiful from her photo, but the person with me in this basement barely resembled her picture. Her rich, dark brown hair was stringy and dirty looking, and her face was drawn with a pasty look to it. Though she was sitting, I could tell she was at least my height, if not a little taller. She was rail-thin, probably from being malnourished. The sweatpants and sweatshirt she wore were at least two sizes too big for her. Either they were Miller's or bought at a K-Mart store. She had on white cotton socks but no shoes.

"Have you taken a shower since you've been here?"

"Every so often he takes me upstairs, but he watches me as I shower." I winced.

"Where do you go to the bathroom?"

She pointed to the pail in the corner. "You need to get us out of here," she said with a pleading look in her eyes.

CHAPTER 55

Why didn't I tell anyone where I was going? Annie knew about the house, but I couldn't remember if I told her where it was. Jesse and Annie were going to be frantic when I don't respond to their calls. It's Wednesday. I just spoke to Jesse so he might not even realize something's wrong for another day or two. Same with Annie. Miller has to leave at some point to go to work. If I could somehow loosen the ropes on my hands, I might be able to get us out of here.

"He's going to kill us," Katie said.

"If he wanted to kill you, you would be dead by now. He wants to keep you as his captive." I didn't want to tell her that when he realizes he no longer needs her, or when he grows tired of her, he will most likely get rid of her. How long before he decides to dispose of me? I had to find a way out of here.

I looked all around trying to find something I could use as a weapon. There was nothing. The basement was completely empty. Katie looked cold. "Are you cold?"

"It's damp in here all the time. I want to go home."

"I know you do." I wanted to distract her. "Tell me what happened? How did you wind up here?"

"How much do you know?"

"I know about Peter Crawford. I just don't know the details."

"You know about Paul?" I nodded. "When I realized how possessive he was, I knew my marriage was over. I met Peter when I was at a bar with my friend Gail. We became involved. At first I didn't know he was married, but when I found out, I didn't care; I didn't want the relationship to end. Jake must have followed us to the motel. He knocked on the door and when I saw it was him, I let him in. I didn't know he was crazy, though I should have figured it out sooner.

"He wanted me to leave with him, but when I refused, he got really angry. Peter tried to intervene and asked him to go, but he wouldn't listen. In a fit of rage, Jake punched Peter, and they began to fight. At one point, Jake picked up the lamp from the table and struck Peter repeatedly on the head. It was horrifying—there was so much blood. I stood there in shock, unable to move. Then Jake grabbed me and threatened that if I screamed, he would kill me. That's when he dragged me into his car, and I was too stunned to react."

"What about Lowell? How did you know he was abusing boys?"

"How did you find out about him?" she said, with a shocked look on her face.

"From your neighbor, Sandra Greene. She didn't want to tell me, but I stressed how important it might be to your well-being."

"It was by accident. We live only a few blocks from each other. I was walking past Lowell's building when I recognized this boy, who's a student where I teach, coming out of Lowell's building. When I asked him what he was doing here, I noticed he'd been crying. I asked him what was wrong, but he said to leave him alone and ran off.

"The next day at school, I approached Lowell and asked him why Oliver was at his apartment and why he had been crying when he left. Lowell mentioned that he tutors Oliver but had no idea why he was crying. I couldn't shake the feeling that something was off. Why would Oliver be upset right after leaving Lowell's place? And why was he being tutored at Lowell's apartment instead of at school or his own home? It just made no sense. The next time I saw Lowell, I confronted him directly. I warned him that if I found out he was doing anything inappropriate with Oliver, I would report him without hesitation."

"Did he threaten you?" I said.

"Not exactly. But I could tell he was very angry."

"It turns out you were right. He was abusing Oliver and another boy named Tommy Jenkins. There's a full police investigation looking into Lowell and he's been suspended. It's good that you mentioned Lowell's first name to Sandra, then I was able to hone in on him. I found the thumb drive at your mother's house, and the police now have those photos."

Katie went quiet. Though she told me what happened, her voice was barely a whisper. It seemed like it was an effort for her to speak. Then I heard it. This scratching sound, but I couldn't figure out where it was coming from. Then I heard it again.

"Katie, I hear these scratching sounds. Do you know what they are or where they're coming from?"

"It's mice. They skitter through the walls."

"Do you ever see them?"

"I hear them mostly at night. One crawled on top of me when I was sleeping. I swiped it away but I was so afraid it would come back and bite me, I couldn't get back to sleep."

I started to sweat and was feeling light-headed. *Please, I can't have an anxiety attack, not now. I have to remain calm for Katie's sake. If I allow fear to take hold, I won't be able to think clearly, and I need my wits about me if we're going to have a chance to get out of here alive. Breathe, keep breathing.* When I looked over at Katie, she was still. It was a bad sign that she stopped talking.

"Katie, I have to ask you something. Why did you send the voice message to your mother instead of your father?"

"Jake was standing over me when I left the message so I couldn't say anything. I thought my parents might sense something was wrong if I sent the message to my mother instead of my father, especially since we weren't on speaking terms."

Time was passing slowly. I was feeling the enormous weight of the situation. I kept trying to loosen the ropes but he had them tied so tight I was having trouble untying them.

"Katie, can you try loosening the ropes on your hands?" She didn't respond. She's been here for more than three weeks and is probably resigned to the fact that she's not getting out. She's given up.

I heard the door open and saw Miller coming down the stairs.

"It's dinner time. Peanut butter and jelly sandwiches. I also have bottled water for each of you," he said, almost as if this was a game.

"I need to go to the bathroom," I said.

"There's a pail in the corner."

"You have to untie my hands."

"No can do. You think I'm stupid. You can pull your pants down with your hands tied."

"Look, Katie isn't doing well. Can you bring her a bowl of soup? She needs more nourishment than a peanut butter and jelly sandwich."

"If I hear one more word out of your mouth, it'll be lights out." And then he disappeared up the stairs.

I was so frustrated and angry at myself as I reflected on my actions. If I hadn't relentlessly pursued Miller, he would have remained oblivious to my suspicions, and I could have quietly rescued Katie from this basement without his interference.

"Please, I just want to get out of here. I feel like I'm suffocating. I can't stop thinking that it's my fault Peter's dead."

"It's not your fault. You can't think like that."

"If I didn't let Jake Miller into the room, Peter might still be alive. I was being selfish."

"We all do things we're not proud of. Listen to me. He chose to be there with you. You didn't force him."

"That sounds good, but you weren't there when that monster was beating him over the head until he was dead." I didn't answer her. I might have felt the same way.

I must have dozed off for a while. With the window boarded up and no light coming in, I had no idea what time it was. Katie was sleeping. I took a bite of my sandwich and realized how hungry I was. I pushed myself up, losing my balance as I tried standing upright. I had no choice but to pee in the pail. Walking was awkward. I gingerly took baby steps. After the whole ordeal was over, I slid down next to Katie.

I whispered, "A friend knows about this house. When she figures out I'm missing, people will come looking for me." Though I sounded confident for Katie's benefit, the reality is that Annie probably had no idea where the house was, and that it was registered under Miller's mother's name. My only hope, if I couldn't find a way to escape, was that Jesse would somehow manage to track me down.

CHAPTER 56

I listened for sounds upstairs, but heard nothing. Had he left, or was he still in the house? I kept glancing over at Katie; she looked listless. I focused on the ropes, trying to loosen them. I hoped he would leave at some point so I could move around, maybe even manage to get up the stairs and push the door open. I knew it would be a long shot, but I had to try. How would I know when he left? Would he even tell us? I was grateful that Katie had a thin mattress to sleep on. I rolled up my jacket and used it as a cushion against the hard cement floor as I lay my head down. How can I be sure what day of the week it was if I couldn't tell day from night down here?

I knew Katie had fallen asleep from her slow rhythmic breathing. As I lay awake, I kept thinking about Jesse and Annie and how worried they would be. I worried that if I couldn't find a way out of here, the walls would be closing in on me. I worried that Katie wouldn't be able to hold on much longer. When sleep finally came, I welcomed it.

***

When I opened my eyes, Katie was still sleeping. I looked up at the boarded window. Unless I was imagining it, there seemed to be a sliver of light coming through. I looked up again and the light was still there. I was relieved that now I'd be able to tell whether it was day or night out. I heard the door open.

"Ah, I see you're finally awake. Here's your breakfast. Don't forget to make sure Katie eats hers," he said, quickly heading back upstairs.

I moved over to Katie. "Wake up. You have to eat to keep your strength up. I need your help if we're going to get out of here." She looked up at me. I fed her the bowl of cereal and milk. "Please drink the water. You have to stay hydrated." After I made sure Katie had breakfast, I ate what he gave me. Then the door opened.

"I'm leaving now, but I'll be back soon. Be good." I never saw it coming. The cloth was over my nose and I was losing consciousness.

When I woke up, I had no idea how much time had passed. I looked up and could see a slight ray of light coming from the window. It was just enough to know it was still daylight. Maybe Miller wasn't back yet. I had to take a chance. I wiggled my way over to Katie.

"Wake up," I said. She started squirming. "Katie, please sit up. I need you to help me loosen the rope on my hands. I can't do anything unless my hands are free. Get up, Katie," I said forcefully.

"Even though your hands are tied, you can still move your fingers. Can you try and loosen the rope?" I could tell she had very little strength in her hands. I kept on encouraging her, but it was no use. Maybe I could try and untie her hands. The problem was that the rope was so thick I couldn't get my fingers around the knot. Using the wall as leverage, I managed to push myself up. If I could reach up to the window, maybe I could yank the board loose. I could hear footsteps walking around upstairs. *He's back.*

The door opened and he ran down the stairs and grabbed Katie.

"Why are you taking her?" I asked, panic rising within me as I realized what he intended to do to her.

"Katie and I are going to have dinner together and spend the night. Would you like to have a shower before you go to bed?" he said to Katie, practically dragging her up the stairs. I could hear her whimpering.

"Take me instead. I'll do whatever you want."

"Maybe next time. I'll be back with your dinner." I felt helpless watching Katie as the door shut behind them.

"Make sure you add a pickle with that peanut butter sandwich," I shouted. I was so frustrated I didn't care what I said.

I sat staring at nothing in particular. There wasn't anything I could do to help Katie. I could only hope she could last a few more days. Somebody will find us, but what if…

CHAPTER 57

I felt exhausted despite having slept a few hours from the chloroform. I could easily drift back to sleep, but I wanted to keep myself awake and not give in to the temptation. The more I slept, the less control I'd have. That can't happen. I knew Miller was feeding us just enough to keep us alive and no more. The door opened.

"Hey, Jake. Why don't I join you upstairs with Katie? Wouldn't that be fun?" I had a feeling he was afraid I would be a threat even though I was incapacitated.

He put down the bowl of soup and kneeled down next to me. "So you want to play, is that it," he said, as he lifted up my sweater and placed his hand inside my bra. "Is this what you want?" I was scared, but I refused to show it. "I know you like how it feels." Maybe because I gave him no resistance he stopped. Though I knew I couldn't show him any fear, I was at his mercy. He had the power to do whatever he wanted to me, and I was completely defenseless to stop him. My body quivered, knowing I wasn't in control. My whole body screamed: *kick him, do whatever you can*, but I was afraid if I did, he would take it out on Katie.

"Eat your fuckin' soup," he said as he got up.

"Where's the ice cream I ordered?" He walked away without a word.

Today is Thursday. Today is Thursday. The light from outside was gone. It was nighttime. What was going on upstairs? What was Jake doing to Katie? *Stop thinking about it or it will drive you crazy.*

When I woke up, Katie was back on the mattress. Her hair looked washed, but she was wearing the same sweatpants and sweatshirt. I managed to push myself up and wobbled over to her. I flopped down and leaned her head against my shoulder. She felt like skin and bones. I was scared for her. I looked up at the window and I could see a shred of light. *Today is Friday. Today is Friday.* By now Jesse and Annie would be frantic. If I knew Annie, she'd already called Jesse.

I waited for Miller to leave. My plan was to take the pail, turn it over onto the mattress, and hopefully reach the window. If I could just use my fingers to loosen the board.

"Good morning, ladies," Miller said, as he came down the stairs with the same breakfast as yesterday; cold cereal and milk.

"Do you think I can get some coffee?" I said with a straight face. He didn't answer me as he went back upstairs, shutting the door behind him.

It seemed like an eternity until he came back down again. I saw the cloth in his hand. When he was close enough, I tried kicking him with my legs and moving my face back and forth. I knew it wouldn't make a difference, but I had to fight back. He slapped me so hard across my face, I could hear my teeth rattle. In the end, I succumbed to unconsciousness.

I woke up to see Katie rolled up in a ball. "Katie, is Miller still gone?" She nodded. "Okay. I'm going to try and reach the window, but I need your mattress."

After a few times trying to get up from the floor, I managed my way over to retrieve the pail and then seesawed my way over to Katie. I gently moved her off the mattress.

"Katie, listen to me. If you hear any noise from upstairs let me know right away. Do you understand?" She shook her head. I took that as a yes. I pulled the mattress under the window and turned the pail upside down. With my feet tied, it wasn't easy getting up on the pail. I had to jump and hold on to the wall to keep my balance and steady myself. After a few tries, I finally managed to stand upright on the pail. My fingers reached far enough where I had enough leverage to grip the board and pull it away from the window. I kept working feverishly, ignoring the pain in my fingers. I had to keep going. I knew that at any moment Miller might be back and wasn't sure when or if I would get another chance. I kept tugging. Every time I thought I was making progress, the board held its ground. Peeking through the slight opening, I could tell the sun was going down. Did that mean he would be back soon?

I was so frustrated that I started banging on the wood board. Did I really think someone was going to miraculously walk by the side of the house, hear the banging through a boarded-up window, and rescue us?

CHAPTER 58

"Noise, noise," I heard from below. I looked down at Katie and saw the panic in her eyes. I quickly jumped off the pail, losing my balance, and falling off the mattress onto the hard cement floor. I frantically scrambled to get myself moving in order to push the mattress back to Katie. It was then that I realized the pail was still on the floor near to Katie. The door opened. There wasn't enough time to get it back on the other side of the room. A chill went through me when I saw the look on Miller's face, his eyes focused on the pail.

"What the hell's going on here?" he said accusingly.

I had to think fast. "Katie wasn't feeling well and was afraid she was going to throw up on the mattress. She thought you would be mad at her, so I brought the pail over here since she's hardly capable of getting it herself."

"Is that true, Katie?" I saw the fear in her eyes. I was hoping Miller didn't notice. Thankfully, she nodded yes.

"How long do you plan on keeping me here?"

"Why, do you have other plans?" he said sarcastically. I didn't answer him. He turned his back to me and went upstairs.

Every part of my body was aching. The fall on the hard floor didn't help, and my fingers were killing me. *Tomorrow is Saturday. Tomorrow is Saturday.* By now, Jesse and Annie would be frantic. My eyes were tearing. It dawned on me that Miller's intentions when he took Katie were to make her suffer because she had rejected him. How much longer before he had his fun and got rid of her? How long before he decided to kill me? I wasn't going down without a fight.

I heard the doorknob turn. Miller was bringing us our delicious dinner. I couldn't wait to see what was on the menu for tonight's supper. My sense of humor was the only thing keeping me going. If I lost that, I knew there was no hope for Katie or me.

I had a peanut butter and jelly sandwich and a bottle of water. What a surprise. I noticed Katie wasn't eating. "Katie, please eat. You need to keep up your strength for when we finally get out of here."

"I can't eat. My stomach hurts."

"You have to try." I knew her stomach was upset because he'd been feeding her garbage for weeks now.

"Please, just leave me alone."

"If I could do this by myself I would, but I can't. I need your help."

"But I'm so tired. I just want to sleep."

"Okay, but first you have to talk to me." I wiggled my way over to her. "Drink a little water. Then take a small bite of your sandwich and I'll do the same." I had to get Katie motivated. Right now she'd given up, and without hope, I was afraid I was going to lose her.

"Everyone I spoke to said you love your students and you love teaching. Tell me about your kids." I wanted to keep Katie engaged; if I could just keep her talking. Katie's eyes were tearing up.

"My kids probably think I abandoned them."

"That's not true. I'm sure Mrs. Roberts told them you had a family emergency and you would be back soon."

"Are you sure?"

"I am. So tell me about your class."

"They're wonderful. I remember my first day of teaching." I got a small glimpse of the Katie before being captured; seeing her face as she talked about her class. "I was petrified. All these little eyes were staring at me. I quickly introduced myself. One of the little boys yelled out, 'you're pretty' and everyone laughed. I guess that was the icebreaker. My first year I had second graders and now I teach third grade. A lot of the kids come from single-parent homes, where most of the parents have to work two jobs. It can't be easy on these kids or the parents."

Katie stopped talking. "What do you like most about teaching?" I said, encouraging her to continue.

"I like to see their little faces when they get excited about learning something new. There's one kid in my class, his name is Eduardo; he's so bright and so eager to learn." Her eyes teared up. "These children bring such joy into my life, and he's taken all that away from me."

I knew she meant Miller. "Listen to me, Katie. I know right now you can't imagine your life having any joy in it, but time will change that. I know from my own experience."

She looked at me. "When I was twelve, my parents died in an automobile crash. I couldn't imagine my life without them; they were everything to me. It took me a long time before I felt something besides sadness and anger. The thing is, without you even realizing it, there will be moments of joy seeping into your life."

"I'm sorry," Katie said.

"Can you tell me another story about your kids?"

"Once, when I was leaving school at the end of the day, I saw that one of the students in my class was waiting outside for her mother, who was very late. The kid was trying her best to be brave, but I could see the tears forming in her eyes. I called the mother, but there was no answer. When she finally called me back, she said she had been exhausted when she came home from work and fell asleep. She never heard the phone ringing. I walked Maria home and her mother swore to me she would never be late again."

"Did she keep her promise?"

"She did."

"When I first joined the police force, I was a beat cop on patrol. I saw this young boy, Felix, standing on a street corner crying. He had begged his mother to allow him to walk to school by himself, but somehow on the way home he got confused and was lost. I can still picture the enormous relief on his mother's face as she saw her son walking toward her."

Katie was falling asleep. I was, too. I wondered if Miller had put something in the water to make us sleepy.

***

It is Saturday. It is Saturday. By this time Jesse and Annie would be beside themselves with worry, frantically trying to find me. I doubt they would be able to locate this house. Why hadn't I told Jesse or Annie where I was going?

"Katie, wake up."

"What's the matter?" she said, barely audible.

I heard footsteps and the door opening.

"Did you girls have a nice sleep? I have your breakfast and a special treat." I saw it was coffee. I was now wondering if he drugged the coffee. At this point I didn't care and drank it very slowly.

"I'll be back in a little while. Katie, you'll be dining with me tonight." I could see the terror in her eyes.

"Katie, would you happen to know if Miller works on Saturdays?" I said, when he shut the door behind him.

"I can't go. I can't go," Katie said, moaning.

"Listen to me. I'm going to try and get us out of here," I said, my voice steady despite the fear coursing through me. "If I can't, when he comes back, I need you to say whatever you can to convince him how sick you are. I'm pretty sure he won't be interested if he thinks you're too sick to be intimate with him." I took a deep breath. "As soon as I hear him leave, I'm going to try and loosen the board again, but first I thought I'd take a crack at the door. That might be easier. Remember, you're my sidekick. I need you to stay strong and trust me." I knew my words were falling on deaf ears. I was afraid if I couldn't get us out today, I wouldn't have another chance.

CHAPTER 59

I wasn't sure how much time had passed when I thought I heard the front door close. I could faintly hear the sound of the engine and a car leaving. A few minutes later, I heard the doorbell ring.

"Help!" I shouted as loud as I could. "We're down here! We're trapped in the basement!" My heart raced with excitement. I pushed myself up and dragged my feet to the bottom of the steps, yelling at the top of my lungs. I sat down on the stairs and began to push myself up, one step at a time, shouting, "We're here! We're here! Call the police! If you can hear me, bang on the door!"

But there was nothing, only silence. "No! No! No!! Please don't leave! Help us!" Panic gripped me. Had they really left? I continued to shout, but as I reached the top step, I realized I didn't know how to stand up without falling back down and injuring myself. I had to try something. I twisted my body to face the door and kicked it with all my strength, hoping it would give way. I kicked again and again, but it wouldn't budge. After a while, I realized the door must be securely locked from the inside.

I maneuvered myself down the stairs and over to Katie. She had been watching the entire time, but when nothing worked, she lay down again without a word.

"Katie, I need your mattress. I'm going to try to get the board off the window again."

"You already tried that," she said without any emotion.

"Katie, I want to get us out of here. Do you understand? I have to keep trying."

"When is your friend coming?"

"I'm sorry, Katie, but I can't wait for someone to rescue us. I don't think we have much time; I doubt he's going to keep us here much longer."

Her eyes opened wide and she recoiled. I didn't know how to get through to her anymore. She seemed resigned to her fate. I seesawed over to get the pail. Katie didn't say anything when I gently slid her off the mattress and placed it under the window. Again, it took several tries to get up on the pail, falling over a few times on the mattress before I finally managed to stand upright.

I was at it so long my fingers bled, but I wasn't going to give up. Every time the board budged ever so slightly my hopes soared, only to have them dashed when it didn't seem to make a bit of difference. The problem was that the board was thick and hard to pull away from the window. I didn't want to give up, but I was afraid Miller would be back soon. I gave it a few more attempts and stopped. It took a while before I was able to get Katie's mattress and the pail back the way they were.

I knew from the little bit of light coming through it was late afternoon. "Katie, do you remember what I told you. When he comes back, say whatever you have to in order to convince Miller you're too sick to go upstairs with him." She didn't respond.

I thought I heard the front door open. A few minutes later, the doorknob turned.

"Have you ladies been behaving yourselves?" he said, with a smug look on his face. Katie remained silent.

"Jake, I think Katie is really sick. She's not moving, and she's white as a ghost. She needs a doctor or else she's going to die." He probably wouldn't care, but I had to say something, hoping he wouldn't take her upstairs.

I was holding my breath. He looked at her and left without saying a word. What did that mean? Now I was worried he'd have no reason to keep us around much longer.

I really believed I could somehow get us out of here, but time was running out. I had no intention of making it easy for him, and I would do whatever it took to fight him off.

CHAPTER 60

I stared into the room, then glanced over at Katie curled up in a fetal position. My thoughts drifted to my parents and how cruel life had been to rip them from me in an instant. I could still hear the echoes of my own screams, trapped inside the car, crying out for my parents, unaware they were gone.

I recalled when I woke up in the hospital. Will's father was holding my hand, tears falling down his face as he looked at me, having to be the one to tell me what happened. Though he wanted to be brave for me, he also lost someone close to him—his brother, my father.

Though I was independent from early on, and virtually raised myself after my parents died, I was a wreck inside. I trusted no one, and as time passed, my fear of loss and enclosed spaces only intensified. Annie was the only person with whom I felt comfortable sharing my thoughts. Despite her patience and willingness to listen, she remained powerless to alleviate my struggles.

The turn of the doorknob interrupted my thoughts. When I saw Miller coming down the stairs, he avoided looking at us and never said a word. He set a bowl of soup down in front of Katie and he gave me the usual peanut butter sandwich and water. He then turned and left.

I scrambled my way over to Katie. I knew in her physical condition and with her hands tied, she wasn't steady enough to lift the spoon to her mouth. What I wanted to do was scream at the top of my lungs, but I didn't want him coming down again.

After we both ate, I tried to get Katie to talk. She just turned her back to me, curled up, and went to sleep. I took her spoon and hid it in my underwear.

It occurred to me that it wouldn't be much longer before he killed us. I was lying down wondering how he was going to do it. Though he said he had a gun, I didn't believe him. He would have threatened me with it when he first threw me in the basement. Once he killed us, he would most likely wait to get rid of our bodies in the middle of the night when none of the neighbors would notice.

I was afraid to fall asleep in case he tried to murder me while I was sleeping. I needed to be awake to have any chance of surviving, even if it was a slim chance.

I was in complete darkness. I kept thinking about Katie's parents and what it would do to them when they found out their daughter was dead. My mind was swirling, all these thoughts running through my head. I thought about the pain my birth mother had to endure all because her religious, God-fearing parents forced her to give up her baby for adoption. She died never knowing I was looking for her. My cheeks were wet. I was fighting to stay awake, pinching myself, but I could feel myself drifting off.

***

I woke up. There was a shred of light in the room. *It is Sunday, it is Sunday*. I looked over at Katie and yelled to her. There was no answer. I heard the doorknob turn. I quickly pushed myself up in a sitting position and reached for the spoon, keeping it out of sight.

His eyes were fixated on me. My heart was beating so fast I thought I would die of a heart attack. I could feel the sweat dripping from every part of my body. I gripped the spoon, waiting for him. As he approached me, all I could see was the icy glare on his face. The intensity in his eyes was terrifying, sending shivers right through me. At that moment he seemed void of any emotion. I started screaming at the top of my lungs.

"Scream all you want. No one can hear you," he said with a sneer on his face.

As he reached down toward me, I just reacted and shoved the spoon in his ear as far as I could. It didn't seem to do much damage, but it made him angry enough to slap me hard across the face. I was momentarily dazed. He grabbed me around the throat, and I bit down on his hand as hard as I could. "You fuckin' bitch," he said, slapping me again. I knew in that instant I was going to die. I tried reaching up to lessen his grip, but his fingers were too tightly wound around my throat. I was barely holding on to consciousness when I thought I heard a really loud noise and then a voice yelling. *Someone is in the house.*

For one quick moment Miller slightly released the pressure. I tried yelling, but no sound came out.

"Maddie, Maddie, are you here? Where are you, it's Annie?" Just then, the basement door swung open. For a moment I thought I was seeing a mirage, my heart racing in disbelief. Before Miller could even react, Annie lunged forward, striking him over the head with a heavy object she had in her hand. I sat there stunned and speechless, as he fell to the ground, out cold.

"Maddie, are you alright?" Annie said, looking terrified as she knelt down next to me.

"Call the paramedics and the police." Katie, who was watching, looked comatose.

Just then, I spotted Jesse coming down the stairs, his face filled with determination. He swiftly pulled out a pocketknife, untying me before tying Miller's hands and feet. Annie helped me up as I struggled to stand. I made my way over to Katie, sinking down beside her. I wrapped my arms around her, holding her tightly, whispering over and over, "You're safe now. He can't hurt you anymore. Help is coming."

CHAPTER 61

I pushed myself up, and when I looked over at Jesse and Annie, they had tears in their eyes. I couldn't believe they were really here.

A moment later I heard Annie talking to someone on the phone. "It's Lucas," Annie whispered. "Yes, she's safe. We'll talk later."

"Do you need to go to the hospital and get checked out?" Annie said.

"I'm okay. I just can't imagine how you found us."

The police and ambulance arrived at the same time. I asked the paramedic where he was taking Katie.

"Give me your phone," I said to Annie.

"Mrs. Peterson, it's Maddie Landon. I want you to know your daughter is safe. The ambulance is taking her to Queens General Hospital."

"Is she alright?" she said, her voice trembling with fear.

"I don't have time to explain now, but she's been through a rough ordeal. Please just meet her there," I said, and hung up.

"I'm Detective Jensen and this is Police Officer Sweeney. What happened here?" he said when they arrived. Detective Jensen's face was stone cold.

"I'm Maddie Landon, a private investigator and former detective with the NYPD. This is Jesse Monroe and Annie Greene, friends of mine. They were able to locate us just as Jake Miller was attempting to kill me. If they had gotten here a few seconds later, I'd be dead.

"Katie Lewis was kidnapped by Miller, the guy lying on the floor. She was held hostage in this basement for several weeks; he raped and tortured her and practically starved her to death. I eventually tracked her whereabouts to this location. When I tried to save Katie, he caught me off guard. He pressed a cloth soaked in chloroform over my mouth, causing me to lose consciousness, and then threw me in the basement. He also killed a man by the name of Peter Crawford."

Officer Sweeney just listened.

I was pretty sure by her nervous demeanor she was a rookie. When I was a newbie with the police force, I was paired with a seasoned detective. Most of my training came from tagging along, learning the ropes, as they say. You don't want to be on the streets without experience. You could be a danger to yourself and your partner.

"You need to come down to the station so we can interview you and your friends and take a statement," Detective Jensen said.

"Look, I'm really exhausted and barely able to think straight. I know you have a lot of questions, but is it possible to take my statement tomorrow? I would be in a better position to answer your questions."

Detective Jensen wanted all of us at his precinct the next day by noon. I knew he would be at the hospital later, hoping to talk with Katie. I was pretty sure she wouldn't be able to answer any of his questions in her condition.

"Detective Jensen, Miller took my phone and I would like to have it back. It must be somewhere in the house.

Can you please try to locate it. Also, I'm not sure if my car has been found yet. My keys must be upstairs, too."

When we got back to my apartment, Lucas was outside waiting for us. They all hugged. I had no idea how Lucas became involved with Jesse and Maddie, but I was looking forward to hearing the story.

"Miss Maddie," Louis said, hugging me. "You gave me a scare. I'm so glad you're alright."

"Thank you, Louis. You're not getting rid of me that easily," I said, with a warm smile.

Jesse opened the door and we all went into the living room. I plopped into my father's chair and everyone else sat on the couch.

I wasn't keen on revisiting what happened in the basement, but I finally pieced together how Lucas connected with Annie and Jesse. Lucas mentioned it was pure luck that he called me to check on my investigation when he did; my phone was dead, raising his suspicions about my well-being. After Lucas learned from my doorman, Louis, that I wasn't home, Lucas asked if he could leave a message for either Annie or Jesse, providing them with his telephone number. He explained to Louis that he had a gut feeling something was off since my phone was dead. Though Louis was initially skeptical, he agreed to let Lucas leave his telephone number. When Louis called my phone and confirmed it was indeed dead, he decided to call Annie using the number listed in my emergency contacts, relaying Lucas's concerns and his contact information.

Before meeting with Lucas, both Annie and Jesse were already aware of my strong suspicions regarding Jake Miller's involvement in kidnapping Katie, prompting them to focus their attention on him. Their first stop was the tennis club, where they hoped to confront Jake Miller, but were met with frustration when they learned he was on vacation and the staff was uncooperative. With only a name to go on and no clear timeline when I had gone missing, they knew they had to act quickly. Jesse diligently checked every database and explored every possible lead, but unfortunately, they soon learned that "Jake" wasn't even his real first name. Despite knowing that Maddie had followed Jake to a house in Astoria, Queens, they were unable to pinpoint the address, leaving them at a dead end. Frustration mounted as they lacked the means to track Maddie's phone. Just as Jesse was considering involving the police, Annie received a call from Louis. Recognizing the urgency of the situation, she quickly arranged to meet with Lucas. Understanding that time was critical, Lucas reached out to his FBI contact, providing my cell number and asking them to track its last known location, hoping it would lead them to me before it was too late.

When Lucas heard from his contact, he called Annie with the location, and without even thinking, Annie raced to her car, calling Jesse as she was driving to the house.

"But how did you get into the house?" I asked Annie.

"I had no choice but to break the bedroom window. I ran to my car and grabbed the tire iron from my trunk. I smashed the window, reached in, and undid the lock. Lifting myself up to get in was the hard part."

"Why didn't you smash the sliding glass door?"

"If Miller was inside, I knew the glass door would make too much noise, giving him ample warning that someone was attempting to break into the house."

I couldn't stop the tears from falling.

"I'm eternally grateful that Maddie met you," Jesse said to Lucas.

"The person who helped me could get into trouble, so let's keep it between us," Lucas said.

"Hey, you falling asleep, babe?"

"I think so. Lucas, do you want to stay here tonight?" I said.

"No, but thanks. Let me know what happens at the police station tomorrow."

"Thank you again. I owe you," Jesse said to Lucas.

"You don't. You're lucky; Maddie's special."

Annie promised to bring lox and bagels for breakfast in the morning. God bless Annie.

CHAPTER 62

I slept straight through until the morning. I showered and was getting dressed when Jesse said, "Hey, get back into bed." I did as Jesse said.

"I thought I might have lost you. You have no idea what Annie was going through," Jesse said. I could hear the frustration in his voice. "I was completely in the dark about what was going on. I should have known where you were going. You put yourself in a dangerous situation, breaking into someone's house you knew could be holding someone captive. Have you any idea how close you came to being killed? It was only sheer luck that we got to you in time."

"Don't you think I know that," I said, tears streaming down my face. "And that's not fair. You could be stepping into a dangerous situation, and I wouldn't have any idea. And don't even try to use the excuse that you're a guy."

"I guess we're even."

"Not even close."

"Very funny," he said as he kissed me, and I was putty in his hands.

A half-hour later, the buzzer rang.

Annie hugged me so tight I thought my ribs would break. I knew that look on her face. It was fear that she could have lost me. I looked away, afraid I might cry.

"I am so famished I could eat every bagel in that bag," I said. Jesse and Annie hugged. While we were eating, I rehashed most of what happened in that basement, leaving out some details that I thought would be too painful for them to hear. I'm pretty sure Jesse wasn't buying all of it, but didn't want to say anything in front of Annie.

***

When the three of us arrived at the station, Detective Jensen escorted us to his office. Detective Jensen was wearing a brown tweed jacket, blue shirt, and khaki slacks. He was close to sixty, about six feet tall with a slight paunch. I noticed pockmarks on his cheeks, most likely from teenage acne. Detective Jensen's office was just spacious enough for a desk, two metal chairs and a steel file cabinet, basically what every detective's room was like. He sat down on a padded swivel chair. A third chair was brought in.

"Here's your phone and keys. Your car was found a few miles from Miller's house. You can pick it up on your way out. Just to let you know, it was completely searched so it might be a little messy."

"Can you tell me if Miller has said anything?"

"He's lawyered up. He was processed and is now being held without bail at the Queens Detention Complex."

"Any possibility he can get out on bail?"

"It depends on the judge, but I doubt it."

"Were you able to speak with Katie?" I said.

"Not yet. I'm going to the hospital later. I did speak with her parents. After seeing Katie, they were pretty shaken up, as you can imagine. Now I want you to disclose to me everything from the very beginning."

I explained to Detective Jensen how I targeted Jake Miller without going into any details about Katie's husband or Gregory Lowell, except to say that Katie had told me that Miller killed Peter Crawford at the motel. I did mention that I knew about the affair and thought someone might have taken Katie from the motel room since her body was never found. I was debating whether to tell him I broke into the house or that the sliding glass door wasn't locked. Either way, I was entering illegally. But in case it went to trial and I was on the witness stand, his lawyer would ask the question. I went with the truth. Jensen kept quiet. The rest of what I told him was exactly what happened in the basement.

We had decided ahead of time what Jesse and Annie were going to tell Detective Jensen. The story goes like this: I had told them I was targeting Jake Miller and mentioned his mother's house in Astoria, Queens, where I thought he might be keeping Katie. When Annie and Jesse finally realized my phone was dead, they knew something was wrong. With what I had told them, they had enough information to track where I was. That's when they broke in and saw Miller as he was strangling me with his bare hands. We left out the part where Lucas called his contact in the FBI to track my phone.

"How did he wind up unconscious?"

"I got to the house before Jesse and hit Miller over the head with a heavy vase that was on a table in the hallway," Annie said. Annie had no choice but to tell Detective Jensen that she broke in through the bedroom window.

"As soon as Katie's able to talk, she'll tell you the horrific torment she suffered every day for weeks. My only regret is that I couldn't get to her sooner," I said.

We had to wait until our statements were typed up. Detective Jensen said he'd be in touch if he had any further questions. I knew we would have to testify if it went to trial.

When I saw my car, I was thankful it hadn't been vandalized. I was definitely going to get it detailed. The idea of driving it, knowing that Miller had been in my car, gave me the creeps. I met Jesse back at the apartment after dropping Annie off.

Later that day, after Jesse and I dropped my car off to get detailed, we went to a neighborhood Italian restaurant that was known for its homemade pasta. As soon as the waiter came over, Jesse ordered a carafe of Chianti.

"You know, you'll do anything to avoid looking at apartments for us," he said, grinning.

"Oh shit. I forgot about Sarah."

"No worries. She called me when she couldn't get hold of you."

"I'm sorry. I can set it up for whenever you have time."

"Let's talk about Lucas," Jesse said.

The waiter came over and we ordered a salad to share. I went with my favorite dish, linguini and clams in a white wine sauce, and Jesse ordered a veal dish.

"I also want to help Lucas," Jesse said. "I'm just not sure he wants our help."

"You may be right. He seems content to be on the streets. I know he wants to see his son, but his ex won't allow it while he's living the way he is."

We were quiet for a few minutes. Our waiter came over with our Chianti.

"To finding an apartment we love," I said, as we clanked our glasses together.

"I'll drink to that. And I want to say I'm sorry I got angry at you before. I know you took a big risk because you care and because you're a great PI. I'm really proud of you."

"Thank you. Neither one of us can predict what can happen in certain situations."

"I was thinking, Lucas can definitely be an asset to you. Do you think the problem is money or that he doesn't want the pressure of living like the rest of us mortals are subject to?"

"What are you getting at?" I said.

"He's told you he's gotten comfortable living on the streets, as weird as that sounds. Now that he's no longer drinking, if he knew he had something to look forward to, it might give him a different perspective. It might give him the motivation he needs to change his lifestyle in order to see his son."

"What are you proposing?"

"I think you might be able to use his expertise in certain situations. He could work for you on an as-needed basis."

"And how would I pay him? I realize the business is growing, but I'm not sure I can afford it yet."

"You would pass on the cost to your client. We do that all the time. When I'm too busy my boss might hire another PI to help with the workload."

"That's a thought, but what makes you think he's going to accept my offer, or even if he does, will it motivate him enough to get off the streets?"

"We'll see. I hope it will."

"On another subject, do you think Miller could get out on bail?"

"That would be shitty, but I doubt it. There are too many charges against him. Not only the murder of Crawford, but the kidnapping of Katie and attempted murder on your life," Jesse said.

Our food came and we ate in silence for a while. I noticed Jesse looking at me.

"What? I know I'm wolfing my food down. It's been so long since I've had anything that tasted so good. I hope I'm not ruining your meal."

"I'm watching you because there's something endearing about the way you eat, even if Emily Post might not approve."

"I'm impressed you know who Emily Post is."

"Look at all the new things you're going to learn about me once we shack up together."

Later that evening, after Jesse and I got into bed, we went after each other like two jackrabbits. When we were exhausted, we lay there, content to hold each other.

"So, do you want to tell me what really happened in that basement?"

I was conflicted. Did Jesse have to know that Miller assaulted me? Every time I think of him touching me, I feel really sick. Do I need to put that image in Jesse's head?

"It was like I told you and Annie. I believe he didn't attempt anything physical with me because he knew I wouldn't put up any resistance. Without that, what would have been the fun in it for him." I wasn't sure if Jesse bought it, but he didn't push me any further.

CHAPTER 64

After Jesse left in the morning, I called Mrs. Peterson.

"We're just on our way to the hospital."

"How is Katie doing?"

"Physically, she's getting better. She's eating a little more each day, but I'm worried about her emotionally. The doctors say it's going to take time. As soon as she feels up to it, they're going to have a psychiatrist come in and talk with her." A moment later she said, "I think she would like to see you."

"I'll come by later today."

After I hung up, I called Lucas.

"Can we meet, say around 5:30 p.m. at the coffee shop? My treat. It's the least I can do for the man who helped save my life."

"Sure. I'm looking forward to the blue-plate special." I laughed, and we hung up.

I picked up my car from the auto body shop where I had brought it in for detailing. When I saw the bill, I wondered if I should include it in my final invoice to the Petersons, but I knew I wasn't going to.

When I arrived at the hospital, I was told to take the elevator to the second floor, Room 205. I opted for the stairs. Before going into Katie's room, I observed Mr. Peterson holding Katie's hand while he was talking to her. Katie was propped up on the bed. I couldn't tell if she was interacting with her parents or just listening. I debated whether to go in or wait a while longer. Mrs. Peterson saw me and waved me in. I was hoping I could be alone with Katie.

When I walked in, I saw the response on Katie's face, her eyes opening wide. Mr. Peterson hugged me, tears in his eyes. "Thank you," he said quietly.

"Hi, Katie." I bent down to give her a hug.

"Why don't we step outside for a few minutes," Mr. Peterson said to his wife. I could see she was reluctant to leave her daughter, but she did as her husband asked.

Not all of her color had returned yet; she still looked quite pale, and when I hugged her, I could feel her delicate frame.

"Thank you," she said, in barely a whisper. "Please thank the people who saved me."

"I will, Katie. They're just glad they were able to get to us in time." I choked up as the words came out of my mouth. "I can only imagine what you've gone through. But I want you to know I'm here for you, and so are your parents and your friends. I know how much they all love you. And don't forget about those kids who need you. I'm going to leave you my card. Please call me any time, day or night."

"Thank you."

Her parents came back into the room. I took Katie's hand and told her I would be in touch. I had no illusions that Katie's road to recovery would be long and hard. Maybe with therapy she could have some semblance of a life.

As I was leaving the hospital, I saw Katie's husband, Paul Lewis, walking in.

"What are you doing here?" I said in an annoyed tone.

"Katie's mother called and told me what happened."

"It doesn't mean you should be visiting her. She's fragile now and doesn't need to be subjected to anyone who's going to upset her. All you've done is make her life a living hell, harassing her like you did. I would think twice about seeing her. If you are so desperate to contact her, why don't you call her in a few weeks when she's feeling better or better yet, NEVER!" I couldn't hold my anger in any longer.

"Maybe I deserve that. I don't know, but I want to thank you for saving Katie."

I didn't answer him. I just walked away. I glanced back for one brief moment to see if he was still there. He was gone. I wasn't sure if Paul Lewis would heed my advice.

When I arrived at the coffee shop, I saw Lucas standing outside. He was wearing a gray sweatshirt and gray sweatpants. His light brown hair, which usually looked tousled, now looked combed. He waved.

"Hey, sorry I'm a few minutes late. Let's go inside. Aren't you cold? It must be forty degrees outside," I said.

"You get used to it."

"I'll take your word for it."

I asked the waitress to seat us in the back booth.

"I noticed you always ask for a table in the back. What's that about?" Lucas said.

"It's from my days on the force. I don't like surprises."

"I had a feeling that was the reason. I think it's the mentality for most of us who have had jobs where danger is involved."

Lucas ordered the meat loaf special, which included mashed potatoes and string beans. I ordered a tuna fish sandwich and fries. I was pretty sure it was Lucas's first meal of the day.

"I was thinking that I might be able to use your brain and skills from time-to-time on my cases. Would you be interested in doing some work for me on an as-needed basis? Of course we'll come to an agreement on the fee. What do you think?"

"Look, Maddie, I don't need your charity if that's what this is. You don't owe me anything. I was more than happy to help."

"You got it wrong, Lucas. I promise you it's not charity. I'm not that generous with my money. I earn every cent that I make, and trust me, I'd rather not share it. But business has been good, and sometimes I have more than one case going on at a time. Though I have a tendency to think I'm supergirl, the reality is there are times when I need help. Also, I know Jesse would love it if I weren't as stressed out as I sometimes am. So, what do you say?"

"You drive a hard bargain, but I accept as long as I'm not busy cleaning up the streets when you need me," he said facetiously.

"Agreed. By the way, I went to see Katie at the hospital and she wanted me to thank you."

"How's she doing?"

"She's been through a horrendous ordeal. I'm not sure how she'll come out of it, but I'm just glad she is surrounded by people who love and support her."

Lucas and I both had coffee and apple pie for dessert. He walked me to my car and gave me a bear hug before we parted. I was deciding whether to say anything to

Lucas about his clothes if he went on any interviews with me, but I thought I would cross that bridge when the time came.

I was ecstatic to be home all by myself. Since my time in the basement, I hadn't been alone. After I undressed and threw on an undershirt, I poured myself a glass of wine and turned on the TV in the bedroom. I propped myself up on the bed. It was the first time I had a minute to relax. I tried not to think about what could have happened to Katie and me if Annie hadn't gotten there in time. It was best not to dwell on it. I sipped my wine and tried to focus on what was on the TV.

CHAPTER 65

The next morning I slept in, which was a luxury for me. It was the first time in months I had nothing on my agenda. I took advantage of it and had a nice leisurely breakfast, leftover lox on a sesame bagel. I was enjoying my second cup of coffee when my phone rang. It was Annie.

"Hey, sweetie," I said.

"You sound relaxed. A minor miracle."

"I am basking in nothingness."

"Some of us don't have that luxury. How are you feeling, really?"

"Why do you have to ask the hard questions?"

"Because I'm a horrible person who loves you, and you can't just ignore what you went through. Maybe you should talk to Dr. Goldberg."

"I'll think about it."

"How about if the five of us go out for a celebratory dinner when Jesse is here? Even though I'm still mad at you for doing something incredibly stupid, I am so proud of you for attempting to save Katie. I can't imagine what it was like for you trapped in the basement with that psycho."

"I like that idea."

"I love you."

"Right back at you."

***

At 5:30 p.m., I was sitting in Dr. Goldberg's waiting room. I realized Annie was right and called Dr. Goldberg after we hung up. Though I was putting on a big front for Jesse, I wasn't dealing very well with what happened. My mind kept going over and over what I could have done differently before I opened the sliding glass door to Miller's house.

"Maddie, come in."

I sat in silence for a few moments and then everything spilled out. Once I started talking, I couldn't stop.

"What you went through was very traumatic. It will take time to process everything that went on in the last week. Can you tell me why you chose to enter that house?"

"Because I was pretty sure Katie was in there."

"Did it occur to you to contact the police?"

"No, I didn't think they would have believed me. Besides, I was afraid by the time they investigated Miller, Katie would be dead."

"Isn't it a possibility they could have knocked and found cause to break in?"

"Maybe, but I didn't think that was likely."

"What's the real reason you didn't call them? Could it have been that you wanted to be the one to save Katie, even if it meant putting your own life in danger? You were entering someone's house illegally. What if he killed you instead of locking you in the basement? What would have happened to Katie?" I had no answer. The thought never occurred to me.

"We talked about this in prior sessions, your need to put yourself in danger. Maybe there was a time when you didn't think about the consequences. You're not that young girl anymore. You have a life worth living. You've chosen a profession you love, but it comes with risks. You have to learn how to confront these emotions where you want to be the heroine."

I remained silent.

"I think we should spend the next couple of sessions talking about what you went through. It's going to take time before you sort out your feelings. From what you've told me, you're blaming yourself for not finding Katie sooner. Unfortunately, our time is up. Instead of waiting a week for your next appointment, I think it would be a good idea to meet this Friday."

I left Dr. Goldberg's office reflecting on how I often put myself in situations without considering the dangers involved. Ever since my parents died, I realized I acted without worrying about the consequences or how my actions would affect others. While I wasn't completely self-destructive, I frequently failed to contemplate the harm my choices could cause to myself or those around me.

When I got home, I pulled out the bottle of Sauvignon Blanc from the refrigerator and drank till I felt numb.

CHAPTER 66

The following morning, I was still hungover from too much wine the night before. I took two Tylenol and was working on my first cup of coffee when the phone rang.

"Hello," I said, trying to sound sort of normal.

"Ms. Landon, it's Sarah Rogers. Did I catch you at a bad time?"

"Would you mind if I call you back a little later?"

"No, of course not," she said. "I'll talk to you then."

I was pretty sure she was calling to find out if I was interested in looking at some apartments, but it felt too soon after everything that had happened. I was still processing my session with Dr. Goldberg. I kept replaying in my mind why I hadn't considered the consequences of entering that house. A terrifying thought crossed my mind: What if I somehow believed I was to blame for my parents' deaths that night? I had never shared with anyone that we were on our way to see a movie I had begged my parents to take me to. Could it be that I had been punishing myself all these years, feeling responsible for their deaths? Tears streamed down my face uncontrollably. When I finally regained my composure, I remembered something Dr. Goldberg said to me—why was it so important that I had to be the one to save Katie? And then it struck me. Maybe it wasn't Katie I really wanted to save, but in my efforts to save her, I was actually trying to save my parents.

I was so exhausted all I wanted to do was sleep. The next thing I knew, it was 2:00 p.m. It was an effort to get up, but I knew if I stayed in bed, I would feel lousy for the rest of the day. I showered and took a walk. I hadn't eaten yet so I stopped at a coffee shop a few blocks from my building. The lunch crowd was gone. The booth in the back was empty and I sat down. After ordering a turkey sandwich, I called Sarah Rogers back.

"Thank you for returning my call. I have an apartment that I think you might be interested in. It's on the West Side in a doorman building, and I'd like you to take a look at it."

I was hesitant about agreeing to see it. "I just don't know when we can. Jesse lives in Connecticut, and I'm not sure he'll be here this weekend."

"Well, why don't you see it first. It can't hurt. If you like it, then Jesse can look at it another day. If it's not right for both of you, then nothing ventured."

The last thing I was in the mood to do was look at apartments. "I won't be able to see it until tomorrow evening," I said, hoping she might not be available then.

"I'll meet you at 6:00 p.m. at the address I just texted you. I'm also sending you the floor plan."

I spent the next couple of hours wandering around the city and eventually found myself in a bookstore browsing the mystery section. I picked up a mystery novel that caught my eye, drawn by its captivating cover and intriguing title.

***

The following day I kept to myself, spending time reading and only speaking to Annie and Jesse. However, I didn't mention the thoughts I had about my parents' deaths. I kept that to myself.

On my way to meet Sarah Rogers, I couldn't shake off the idea of Jesse and the notion of moving in together. A small voice inside me kept saying: "Turn around, it's not too late." *What is wrong with me? I'm crazy about Jesse.* I kept walking until I suddenly realized it was drizzling, the rain coming down heavier with each step I took. I pulled the hood of my sweatshirt up to avoid getting soaking wet. I was two blocks from the building when I thought I heard footsteps behind me, but when I turned around, no one was there. My nerves had been shot ever since Miller almost killed me. I kept on walking, but suddenly I felt a knife at my throat. Before I had time to react, I was pulled from the street into an alleyway.

With my right elbow, I shoved as hard as I could into Gregory Lowell's stomach. He bent over, the knife releasing from my neck. I turned around, but he was quick, lunging at me as I sidestepped in the nick of time while the knife grazed my jacket.

I reached down and grabbed my gun from my ankle holster. "Stay back," I warned, my voice steady.

"You won't shoot me," he replied, a smirk playing on his lips, but I could see the flicker of doubt in his eyes.

"I will if I have to," I shot back, my heart racing. "You don't want your life to end this way."

"My life was over once the police arrested me." In a desperate move he charged at me, knocking my gun out of my hand. We struggled on the ground, the knife dangerously close to my face. Panic was setting in but I pushed it down. Out of the corner of my eye, I saw my gun on the ground, only a few inches from my grasp. The adrenaline in my body was taking over, my fingers stretching to reach for the gun. In an attempt to intercede, he went for it, but I was faster. I grabbed hold of my gun and pulled the trigger. Lowell fell on top of me. I pushed him off as fast as I could. When I looked down, I saw I was covered in blood. I quickly felt for his pulse, but there was none.

I spotted someone near the alley and shouted for them to call the police. I just sat there, my mind and body numb, struggling to comprehend what just happened. I covered my eyes, overwhelmed by the weight of my actions. Even as a police officer, I had never taken a life. The thought made me sick to my stomach. Why did he have to come after me? Why wasn't he in jail?

I heard sirens. Soon they would be here. I knew I had to call someone, but who? A minute later, two police officers were standing over me, guns pointing at my face.

"I'm not armed, my gun is on the ground."

"Maddie Landon, is that you? It's Detective McFarland." I felt both surprise and relief at the sound of his voice. He had worked out of the same precinct as I did when I was on the force.

"It was self-defense," I said quickly. "Please call Detective Brian Griffin at the 9th Precinct. Inform him that Gregory Lowell attacked me. I had no choice—I had to shoot him. He was going to kill me."

The ambulance came and pronounced Lowell dead.

"I'm going to have to take you into the station and take your statement. Even if it was self-defense, we still have to do a thorough investigation. I know you understand the procedure. I would suggest you call a lawyer before you say anything else."

As we drove to the station, I called Larry Banks, the criminal defense attorney who works in one of the offices on my floor. He said he would meet me at the station. I then called Jesse. I was having trouble talking since I was still in shock. He told me he was not far from the city and would meet me at the precinct.

"Don't worry, everything will be fine."

I wasn't as confident as Jesse, even though I knew I hadn't done anything wrong. Terror seized me, causing my entire body to tremble. I understood all too well that even innocent people could be arrested.

I knew the drill. When we got to the station, Detective McFarland brought me into the interrogation room and told me the interview was being taped.

"Do you want to wait till your lawyer gets here?"

"What I want to know is why he was out on bail? I was told he didn't have the money to make bail."

"I can't answer that right now. I don't know. Why don't you tell me what happened."

There was a knock on the door. It was Larry Banks.

"Did you say anything yet?"

"No, but I have nothing to hide."

"Is she being charged with anything?" Banks asked.

"Not at the moment. We just need to take her statement to find out what happened. As you know, after we complete our investigation, it's up to the district attorney's office whether charges will be filed."

"I'll stay here while Maddie gives her statement."

"No problem."

"Go ahead, Maddie," Detective McFarland said.

I began by explaining how I discovered that Lowell had abused Oliver Seaver, concluding with the moment he attempted to kill me. By the time I had finished my statement, I just wanted to go home, but I knew McFarland had more questions.

"Maddie, I'm sorry for everything you went through. Were there any witnesses to what happened earlier?"

"I have no idea. I spotted someone near the alley and shouted for them to call the police. I'm not sure how long they had been watching."

"Okay. Now tell me again what happened this evening."

"Maddie, you don't have to say another word," Banks said.

"If I don't, they'll think I have something to hide and I don't."

I went over how Lowell first had a knife at my throat to when I pulled the trigger.

"He didn't give me a choice. I warned him to stay back but he wouldn't listen. If I hadn't pulled the trigger, he would have killed me. It was him or me."

"Are you sure there was nothing else you could have done? Weren't you angry that he sexually abused the boy? Was that going through your mind right before you pulled the trigger?"

"What are you saying?" Larry Banks interjected.

"I'm just posing the question."

"No, you're not. I think we're done here," Banks said. "If you have any further questions, please contact me."

As we were walking out of the police station, I saw Jesse coming toward me. Without saying a word, he held me as my body shook. When we let go, Jesse and Larry Banks introduced themselves.

"I spoke to Detective Griffin on my way over," Banks said. "He told me he had just found out a few hours ago that Lowell made bail. He was released yesterday."

"So what happens now?" I said, even though I knew what he was going to say.

"After the investigation is completed, the district attorney's office will review the evidence, the witness statements, and the circumstances surrounding the incident. If they conclude that your actions were justified as self-defense, they will, in all probability, decide not to file any charges.

"Listen, Maddie, there's nothing there. They'll do their investigation and then clear you. I don't want you to sit home and worry. I'll follow up with McFarland just to keep an eye out," Banks said. "Get a good night's sleep."

I was pretty sure sleep wouldn't come anytime soon.

CHAPTER 67

"Jesse, I'm scared," I said when we were lying in bed. "What if they rule it wasn't self-defense? I know how the system works. I've seen it firsthand. McFarland was trying to provoke me, trying to get me to say I was angry at Lowell and wanted him dead."

"That's his job. You know that."

"That doesn't make me feel any better. Shit, they're going to interview everyone involved, including poor Katie who's still fragile. She's already been questioned about what Miller did to her, now they'll question her regarding Lowell.

"Do you realize if they think they have enough to file charges, I could lose everything—my business, my reputation. Even if I'm found innocent, no one will hire me."

"I know whatever I say won't make you feel better, but please remember, you had no choice."

"But maybe I did. Could I have shot him in his leg or arm? Maybe McFarland was right. I was angry at Lowell for what he did to those kids. I did want to kill him."

"But you wouldn't have. The only reason you did was because he was going to plunge a knife into you. You were trained to shoot at a large mass and that's what you instinctively did. You aren't thinking rationally now. You're second-guessing yourself and I won't allow that to happen. We will get through this together. Right now you have to take care of yourself."

"What am I supposed to do?"

"What you normally do—go for your usual run in the morning or to the gym. See Annie, go to the movies. You can still work. I know you believe you can't, but I assure you, you can. Maybe spend more time at my place. I can take time off."

"I'd be terrible company."

"Let me worry about that."

"Oh shit!" When I finally looked at my phone, I saw that Sarah had left several messages.

"What?"

"I didn't want to say anything in case I didn't like it, but I was on my way to meet Sarah when Lowell attacked me. She had an apartment she wanted me to see."

"You'll call her in the morning."

"Listen, I don't think this is the right time to make any decisions about apartments. Everything is too uncertain." Though he tried to hide it, I could see the disappointment on Jesse's face.

"You have to understand, I feel my world is falling apart. It's still hard for me to believe I took someone's life and everything I've worked for may be in jeopardy."

"When I think about how close you came to dying again…"

"But I didn't," I said, holding Jesse close to me.

We eventually fell asleep wrapped in each other's arms.

***

In the morning I told Jesse to go back to work. I knew he wanted to be here for me, but the truth is, I wanted to be alone for a while.

"I'll come up to you in a day or two. By then I won't feel so overwhelmed." That probably wasn't true, but I needed to be by myself for now.

"I understand, but I'm not going to allow you to push me away."

"I won't. I promise."

Jesse left a few hours later. I was sitting in the living room, staring at nothing. The phone startled me. It was a wrong number. The next time it rang, it was Annie. I debated whether to pick up, but I knew she wouldn't stop calling if I didn't.

"Let me guess, Jesse called you."

"Never mind that. I'll give you a choice. I can come over after work or you can meet me at The Dead Poet. NO is not an option."

"And if I say no?"

"I'll come over and bang on your door until you let me in. By the way, you do realize I have a key to your apartment?"

"I'll see you there at 6:00 p.m."

When I looked at the time, it was 3:00 p.m. The bottle of Cabernet Sauvignon was sitting on my kitchen counter. I kept staring at it. I knew I was feeling sorry for myself but I didn't care. Why didn't he listen to me? Did he want me to kill him?

I kept staring at the bottle, my mind reliving every moment of last night. I knew Jesse said I had no choice, but the words of Detective McFarland kept echoing in my head: "Are you sure there wasn't anything else you could have done?"

I took a shower and left my apartment. I walked aimlessly around the city. I knew if I went down the rabbit hole I wouldn't get myself out. My phone buzzed; I saw it was my birth father.

"Hi, Harris!" I said, trying to sound upbeat.

"Hi, Maddie. I was thinking about you earlier. I may be coming to New York on business in a couple of weeks and I thought we could spend some time together."

At that point I lost it. I started crying and couldn't stop. People were staring at me.

"Maddie, what's wrong?" he said when I finally stopped crying.

I sat down on a park bench and told my father everything that had happened in the last couple of weeks. "I could lose everything."

"That's a possibility but I doubt it."

"But without my work I don't know who I would be. I love what I do, and I'm afraid what will happen if they charge me."

"I know you're feeling overwhelmed right now, and I completely understand. However, please allow yourself some time to process things when your emotions aren't so fresh."

"Thank you. I'll try."

"How are Jesse and Annie?"

"Good. Jesse and I were looking at apartments, but after what happened, I told him it would have to wait until a decision has been made by the district attorney's office."

"How did he react?"

"I think he was a little disappointed, but he understands."

"Keep in mind that the last couple of weeks you've been through hell. Cut yourself a break. I promise it will get better. Just remember, I'm only a plane ride away. I'll always be there for you." I felt a lump in my throat as I said goodbye.

CHAPTER 68

Annie was waiting outside The Dead Poet when I arrived. She gave me a ferocious hug. The hostess seated us right away. When the waitress came over, we both ordered a glass of Malbec.

"I'm not going to say anything, just that I love you and you look like shit."

"Thanks a lot." I couldn't help but give Annie a little smile. I took a big gulp of my wine as soon as the waitress placed it down on the table.

"Annie, I'm frightened. What if they charge me?"

"I know I'm the upbeat and positive member of this group, but you have to stop this. Look at it rationally. Did he give you a choice? The answer is no."

"But there were no witnesses. They just have my word."

"You don't know that. If you want to sulk until they come back with a determination, that's up to you. But what is the upside to that? You know, I think I'm going gray just worrying about you," Annie said, chuckling.

"I wouldn't want that to happen. I could use another drink."

Annie called the waitress over and ordered two more Malbecs with sliders and chicken skewers.

"I think I'll spend a few days with Jesse. Getting away from the city might be good for me."

"Do you remember the time when we were walking home from school and decided to take a shortcut through an abandoned lot? I think we were in the ninth grade. We ran into these two cocky boys who thought they were real tough guys. They were taunting us, saying stuff like we're stupid, or where did you get those ugly clothes. Then one of them got really aggressive and tried to open my blouse. Before the kid realized what was happening, you pounced on him, giving him a bloody nose. The kid started crying and his friend ran away, leaving him on the ground. You told him if he ever came near us again you'd not only give him a bloody nose, but you'd put him in the hospital."

"I do remember that. Is there a point to the story?"

"There is. You're tough and you're a fighter. And don't forget that."

CHAPTER 69

In the morning I woke up with a headache from one drink too many. I wanted to call Larry Banks but I knew there was no point since they had just started the investigation. It could take weeks, if not longer, before they made a determination. From my point of view, what the hell was there to investigate? But I knew McFarland would do his job and talk to everyone who was connected to both Lowell and me.

I was on my second cup of coffee when I saw Jesse was calling.

"How's my favorite girl," he said when I picked up.

"I think that was a sexist remark."

"Glad to hear you still have your sense of humor; one of your most endearing qualities, among many others."

"Now you're just trying to flatter me with bullshit."

"You see right through me. When are you coming up?"

"I was thinking tomorrow. Don't worry. I don't plan on jumping off any bridges yet."

"Great. I love you. See ya soon."

As I was hanging up, my phone rang. I saw it was Lucas. It occurred to me that he had no idea what happened with Gregory Lowell.

"Hi, Lucas."

"I can tell by your voice something's not right." How the hell does he do that?

"Remember me telling you about this guy Gregory Lowell who I found out had been abusing boys at his school? Well, he was arrested, and when he was out on bail, he tried to kill me, though lucky for me, I wound up killing him."

"Whoa! What happened from the beginning?"

I went through everything, including the fact that there was now an investigation into his death. "At this point there's nothing I can do until the district attorney's office makes its decision. If they decide to arrest me, I could lose everything."

"Are you doing anything right now?"

"You mean besides filling my day with worry and walking the streets?"

"I'm hungry. Why don't we get something to eat. I'll even leave my stomping ground and meet you wherever you say."

"I'll see you at the coffee shop."

Lucas was waiting outside when I got there. His hair was combed and looked recently washed. He had on a different set of clothes, khakis and a light brown shirt, though the jacket he was wearing didn't look warm enough for end of November weather. This was probably the first time Lucas was better groomed than me. I barely took a shower, and I couldn't make the effort to wash my hair. We took the booth in the back of the coffee shop.

"This Detective McFarland is pretty thorough. I just can't figure out how they can come to any other conclusion but self-defense," I said.

"Unless there's a witness who saw what happened and said you used undue force, there's no way they can hold you accountable. Because you were a former police detective with the NYPD, this detective doesn't want the appearance of favoritism so he's being overly cautious."

"I hope you're right, but it felt strange knowing Lowell was there to kill me. There was a moment when I had the upper hand and offered him a chance to back off, yet he refused to take it, making it clear that he was determined to follow through with his intentions."

"In his mind, going to prison as a pedophile is practically a death sentence. He would have been tortured and sexually assaulted in prison."

"You're probably right."

When the waitress came over, Lucas ordered scrambled eggs, bacon, and home fries with an English muffin and coffee. I realized I hadn't eaten much in the last few days and was kind of hungry. I ordered French toast, bacon crisp, and coffee.

"Have you spoken to your son recently?" I asked Lucas.

"Yeah. Each time we get on the phone, he reads me pages from a book called *The Lucky Baseball Bat*. It's about a young boy who moves to a new town and has a passion for playing baseball. He inherits a baseball glove and bat, which he uses to play on a Little League team and winds up helping the team win the championship."

"Does Max play on a Little League team?"

"He does. I would go and watch him play, but the baseball field is in Rye, where he lives with his mother. Even if I could take the train, I would then have to take an Uber to get to the baseball field."

"Next time there's a game, let me know and we'll go." Though Lucas avoided my eyes, I could see he was moved by what I said.

"I'm going up to Jesse's for a few days. I'll just drive myself crazy if I stay here." I didn't mention the nightmares that wake me up in a panic.

"If you need me for anything, just call," Lucas said.

"Thanks."

Since I never made it to my appointment with Dr. Goldberg last Friday, we rescheduled for today at 5:00 p.m.

***

"Come in, Maddie."

"How are you feeling?" When I spoke to Dr. Goldberg on the phone, I had shared the bare bones of my encounter with Gregory Lowell.

"I'm petrified that I could lose my license and the profession I love. If they decide to charge me, even I'm not convicted, I doubt anyone will hire me. I'd be finished."

"Why don't you tell me what happened."

I went through what transpired that night. "I didn't want to kill him, but he gave me no choice."

"You took someone's life. What you're feeling is completely understandable. It's not uncommon to feel guilt even though you did nothing wrong. Those feelings can be overwhelming, questioning what, if anything, you could have done differently."

"I feel like I'm being punished for my actions. Now I just have to wait to see what the district attorney's office is going to do. It's like being trapped in a nightmare that you can't wake up from."

"Maddie, healing from such a profound experience will take time, and talking about it here will help you to process the emotions you're feeling. It's also important to allow people close to you to help, and not push them away. I think for the next couple of weeks we should see each other twice a week." I nodded in agreement.

CHAPTER 70

The next day, I drove up to Jesse's place in Chester, Connecticut. I hadn't been there in a while, given everything that had been going on.

Jesse wound up taking some time off from work. Though he was trying to be subtle, I knew he was doing everything he could to make sure I kept my mind off what was looming ahead of me. Between bicycling around town, hiking, and taking rides in the area, there was no time to dwell on what happened. We tried playing chess, but I couldn't concentrate. Thankfully, Jesse had filled the wine rack.

One afternoon, we picked Leo up from school and took him to an indoor arcade. I'm not sure who enjoyed playing the games more, Leo or Jesse.

At night, I took out all my anger and frustrations when we made love. Jesse was just along for the ride, though I'm sure he was fine with it. We kept our conversations to the present, keeping future plans out of our discussions.

I left three days later. The drive back was slow going, my mind wandering, one moment doubting the decisions I'd made over the past few weeks, and the next minute thinking about what Annie said—did I have the mental strength to fight my demons. What I wanted to do was sleep until the nightmare was over.

***

The next two weeks went by slowly. I tried to keep busy. I ran a lot and even went into the office a few times, mostly staring at the ceiling. I had a few clients call me for various searches. I told them it might be a few days before I got to it. Though they weren't happy about it, they didn't take their business elsewhere.

I kept mostly close to home. Annie came over a few times, mostly to check up on me. Cousin Will called several times to make sure I was still alive and hadn't done anything foolish. Jesse came on the weekend, and we mostly hung out in the apartment.

At one point I couldn't stand it anymore and called Larry Banks. He told me he had spoken to the assistant district attorney and was told the investigation was wrapping up, but wouldn't tell him anything about their decision.

Now that I knew a decision was imminent, I felt increasingly tense. With no control over the situation, I was barely sleeping and eating. I had been seeing Dr. Goldberg twice a week, and although the nightmares persisted, I was gradually processing what had happened that night.

This morning, I woke up with the decision to visit my parents' graves, hoping that being there would give me some comfort. I drove to the cemetery in Queens. Since I had visited them multiple times, I easily located their graves. Scott and Melissa were just thirty-eight years old at the time of their passing. I brought a blanket to sit on, knowing the ground would be cold.

"Hi, Dad, hi, Mom. I miss you both every day and wish you were here with me right now. I'm so scared. What

if they think I had a choice and that I didn't have to kill him? Dad, you always knew the right words to say when I was afraid. What would you tell me now? Annie says I'm a fighter, and you always taught me to be strong and believe in myself. I'm trying, but I feel like I have no control over this situation. I promise to let you know what happens. I love you both so much."

I sat in my car with the engine running, the heater blasting to keep me warm. When my phone rang and I saw it was Larry Banks, my heart raced. *What if they decide to charge me? Maddie, breathe. You're a fighter; you'll get through this.* With trembling fingers, I answered.

"Hi, Maddie, it's Larry. They've made a decision…"

THE END

Thank you for reading my novel. As an author your feedback is invaluable. I would appreciate your taking the time to leave a review wherever you purchase your books.

ACKNOWLEDGMENTS

Growing up I had an affinity for reading mystery books. I guess choosing to become a private investigator shouldn't have surprised me. Working in the field has provided me the opportunity to use my skills and knowledge to write the books I enjoyed reading growing up.

Bringing my protagonist, PI Maddie Landon, to life has allowed me to craft stories that I hope will captivate my readers to follow Maddie as she navigates both her personal and professional life.

My heartfelt gratitude to my wonderful friends for their love and support. A special thanks to everyone who has contributed to the writing of this book, including Alexa Recio and Siobhan Mitchell for their invaluable input. I also want to thank my friend Sue and my daughter Carrie for taking on the task of reading my pages and providing me with their insights.

I want to give a big thank you to the team at BooksGoSocial for their patience and assistance throughout the completion of my book. Additionally, I am grateful to IndiesUnited for their support in publishing it.

I would like to express my thanks to the Scarsdale Library and The Formosa Coffee in Scarsdale, along with everyone associated with these wonderful places, for proving me the space to write this novel.

Most of all, I want to thank all my readers. I hope you have enjoyed reading my book as much as I enjoyed writing it.

ABOUT THE AUTHOR

As a private investigator with more than thirty years of experience, Ellen Shapiro's professional expertise has brought an authenticity to her characters and the storylines she has created for her novels. Acting on her passion for writing, she enrolled in the Sarah Lawrence Writing Institute where she took courses in creative writing.

Ellen has written articles in her field for both local and nationwide newspapers and is the author of seven mystery novels. Ellen is a member of Mystery Writers of America and resides in Scarsdale, New York.

Author website: eshapiropi9.wixsite.com/ellen-shapiro
Facebook: @facebook.com/ellen.shapiro.948
Twitter: @twitter.com/EllenShapiro10
Instagram: @instagram.com/eshapiroauthor